AJ and Friends

AJ and Friends

The Discovery

CHERYL WYLIE-HARVEY

iUniverse, Inc.
Bloomington

AJ and Friends
The Discovery

iUniverse books may be ordered through booksellers or by contacting:

iUniverse
1663 Liberty Drive
Bloomington, IN 47403
www.iuniverse.com
1-800-Authors (1-800-288-4677)

ISBN: 978-1-4620-1574-0 (sc)
ISBN: 978-1-4620-1572-6 (hc)
ISBN: 978-1-4620-1573-3 (ebk)

Library of Congress Control Number: 2011960044

Printed in the United States of America

iUniverse rev. date: 11/30/2011

Contents

Dedication

For my family: My husband, best friend supporter and encourager, Stephen, for our daughter Amy and her family, Shawn, Cassidy and Ashley, for my son Eric and his wife Liza, and last but not least, for my granddaughter, AJ—remembering the hours we spent when she was growing up inventing stories and dreaming about talking dogs.

Forward

This book was written to entertain; first, to entertain my granddaughter and her friends, and then at the urging of friends and family, to entertain a wider audience. I've done something completely against the rules: I've used the real names of family members and a few friends—because, after all, everyone wants their fifteen minutes of fame. So, the good guys are real, St. Paul church is a real church in Largo, Florida, and Max is a real canine member of the Harvey family. However, the rest of the story is pure imagination, like terrorists in the neighborhood—that could never happen in the US. At least that's what we thought until 911.

Some people think this book might be too scary for middle school age kids, but I think we live in a scary world, and these kids already know that. I love this age group of kids, they're bright, savvy and a lot more world aware than my generation was at their age. I hope you will all love the adventures of AJ, Khristian and Max. (Of course the real Max can't talk, or can he?)

Acknowledgements

Thanks to my good friend, Carol Cummings for the many hours of reading, rereading, editing and encouraging, and my new friend, Jim Puyda for his exciting art work. God bless you both.

Scavenger Hunt

AJ can't believe her luck. This has to be the best escape from punishment in the history of the world. She hurries to the phone, her faithful dog, Max, following close on her heels. At seventy-pounds, Max is part collie and part German shepherd, but he looks more like an Irish setter, only bulkier. Well, make that fatter. AJ's grandma calls him coffee table because she says his back end is so wide she could put a plant on it. But Max is a handsome, brownish-red with a black muzzle, and intelligent brown eyes. He and AJ are BFFs.

"K, guess what? You'll never guess. Never in a million years. Try to guess, anyway. But you'll never guess. Not even if I give you fifty clues. Not even if you'd been listening in. Not even if I gave you a hundred clues. I bet you can't guess, can you?"

"I might be able to, if you'd take a breath and give me a chance," was Khristian's sardonic reply. Khristian was twelve, a year older than Alyssa, and he never seemed to get too excited about anything.

"Sorry. I'm doing it again, aren't I?" AJ answered.

"It's OK, Jabbermouth. I'm used to your never-ending sentences."

"Don't call me that. I hate it when you call me that."

"Then don't talk so much, and don't talk so fast. What's up, anyway? When I talked to you after school, you were afraid your mom was going to ground you for getting a bad grade. Did you hide that note from your teacher?"

"No, I didn't hide the note. If I did that and my mom found out, I'd really get in trouble. But you'll never guess what happened."

"Just tell me, Alyssa." Alyssa J. Renae Harvey, known to everyone as AJ, was a sunny child. Her long blond hair, big blue eyes and ready smile that displayed big dimples, quickly won her many friends. Well, they used to, anyway.

"Well, Mom asked me why I'd gotten such a bad mark, and I couldn't help it. I started crying."

"Just like a girl."

"I am a girl."

"Yeah, but you don't usually act like one."

"Very funny! Do you want to know what happened or not?"

"Go ahead, I'm listening."

Max was looking up at AJ, and he seemed to be following her end of the conversation. He tilted his head and even whined at times.

"Whatever. Mom asked me what was wrong, and I finally told her how unhappy I am in my new school."

"I thought you weren't going to tell her."

"I wasn't, but I was upset and it just sorta popped out. I feel bad that my mom is spending so much money to send me to this private school, but I had to tell her." AJ's eyes filled with tears just talking about it. She swiped them away with her hand.

"Take a deep breath. If you start crying, I'm hanging up."

AJ took a deep breath and started over. "I told Mom how none of the kids at school talk to me, and how I eat lunch by myself every day. I told her I don't have one single friend there."

"What did she say?"

"She asked if the kids are mean to me. But they're not. You know I've told you that. They're not nasty to me, they just ignore me. It's like I'm not even there."

"So what did your mom say?"

"This is the part you're not going to believe. She said a lot of stuff about my grades being my responsibility and stuff like that, typical Mom stuff. But then Mom said she thought it might be a good idea if I have a Halloween party. She said I can invite kids from my old school, kids from our bowling team and youth group, and kids from my new school. She said that once they get to know me, I won't have any problems making friends."

"Wow! How did you pull that off? I thought you were going to get grounded, for sure. Now you get to have a party?"

"Yeah, can you believe it? And it's going to be a costume party. Mom said my grandma knows lots of great games we can play, and we'll have a costume judging, and eat pizza, and even have a scavenger hunt . . . she said . . .". Max stood up and barked, as if he were as excited as AJ.

"Whoa! Slow down. Your mouth is racing again."

"Khristian, sometimes you make me so mad." The kids talked about the party for a while and even decided they would dress as Harry Potter and Hermione Granger. Khristian loved Harry Potter.

Later, Max jumped up on her bed while AJ was getting her pajamas on. She sat on the bed and hugged the dog. "Max, I'm so happy. I still can't believe it. I get to have a party. Isn't that great?" AJ always talked to Max like he could understand everything she said and like he just might answer her back. Maybe she had some intuitive knowledge about the adventure they were just beginning.

"I'll never understand adults, will you, Max?" Max rolled over for AJ to scratch his belly. "Is that a no?" AJ said and laughed. She rubbed Max's tummy for a while, then lay down next to him with her fingers intertwined behind her head to think about the party. Max lifted his head and gave her cheek a big, wet, sloppy kiss. He sure loved his human.

The night of the Halloween party arrived warm and humid—a typical Florida October night. The family decorated the entire front yard and the front of the house. A huge spider web with a gigantic green and black

3

striped spider dangled from the garage eave. Bats and glow-in-the-dark skeletons shimmered from every surface. A fog machine spewed murky vapor, and an old tape player screeched from the window sill.

Only Max wasn't cooperating. AJ was trying to put a tutu on him. It was left over from when she used to play dress up as a little girl. "Max, stand up. I want to put this on you," AJ complained. But Max stubbornly sat right where he was. It's not easy to dress a 70 pound dog if he doesn't cooperate.

"What are you doing?" Khristian asked. AJ explained that she wanted Max to be dressed up for the party and Khristian roared. Max growled at him.

"Hey, down boy! I don't blame you. I wouldn't wear it either," Khristian laughed.

AJ finally gave up on her dog. "Fine, you can't be in the costume judging then."

"Yes he can," Khristian said. "He can pretend he's a dog." Max growled again.

The kids began arriving, and they naturally separated and stood in four distinct groups. The kids from St. Marks, AJ's new school, stood near the fog machine. The St. Paul church youth group kids chose the punch bowl, while the kids from her old school and her bowling friends stood on the porch and driveway. AJ made the rounds to each group of kids and tried introduce them to one other; but with twenty-four kids attending the party, it wasn't easy.

There were plenty of chaperones, including AJ's Aunt Liza, pronounced Lisa, who taught first grade, and her Uncle Eric who was a sheriff's deputy. Her great Uncle John and Aunt Cathy were there, and, of course, Mom, Mema and Papa. Uncle John and Aunt Cathy brought their three-year-old granddaughter, Jamie. She was running back and forth between the groups of kids and making a major pest of herself. Hosting the party was a family affair.

AJ went into the house to look for her grandmother, and found her refilling the punch. The punch bowl was a black cauldron with a ghostly hand made of ice sticking out of its center. Mema made the hand by filling a rubber glove with water and freezing it. It was pretty cool looking. She and AJ also made ice cubes the old-fashioned way, in trays. They put either a plastic bug or an eyeball in each of the tray compartments before they filled them with water and froze them. Every ice cube had a surprise in it.

"Meems, what are we going to do? All the St. Mark kids are only talking to the other St. Mark kids, the kids from bowling and church are with the other kids from bowling and church, and the kids from my old school . . . , well, they're just not mixing at all."

"Don't worry, sweetie. I have an idea how we can fix that. Is everyone here?"

"I think so."

"Great! Let's take this punch out and start the games."

Outside, Mema blew a big silver whistle (like the coaches at school use) and told the kids to gather around. She said, "You might get wet or messy with some of the games we're going to play, so we're going to judge costumes first." Mema lined all the chaperones up at one end of the circular driveway and had the kids parade around and around past them. Three kids floated by in Scream costumes, and Joe and his twin sister Justine were Thing One and Thing Two, complete with red and white stripped pajamas and blue hair. Allie wore a neat 50s poodle skirt and saddle shoes, Cody was a mad doctor, and Sarah and Morgan were the Blues Brothers. No one could figure out what Nick was supposed to be. An older neighbor girl, who thought she was Gothic, came as herself. Joe and Justine were the unanimous winners.

After the kids changed out of their costumes into some old clothes, Mema blew the whistle again and had them count off from one to three. She put the ones on a team, the twos on a team and the threes on a third team. That way, the three teams each had kids from the four groups attending the party.

Papa put three buckets filled with ice-cold water at the top of the driveway and three empty buckets at the bottom.

"One person from each of the three teams will fill up a coffee can from the bucket at the top of the driveway, run down the driveway and dump the water into the empty bucket. Then you'll run back up the driveway and pass the coffee can to the next team member and go to the end of the line. We'll time you for five minutes."

"That sounds too easy," Khristian said.

"Well, there is a catch. The coffee cans have holes punched in the bottom, so you'll need to move fast to get to the other bucket with any water left in your coffee can." Everyone was groaning and laughing in anticipation of getting soaked.

"When I blow the whistle again, start running." That game was a lot of fun, and the kids learned each other's names so they could cheer on their team members. One of the groups even allowed little Jamie to play on its team. Max ran up and down the driveway at first, chasing the running kids and barking. But Max was overweight and pretty lazy, so he was soon lying at the side of the driveway, just watching, his head going back and forth like watching a tennis match.

Mema ran down the driveway with Jamie when she took her first turn, to show her what to do. But Mema's kind of pudgy too, like Max, and by the time they got back to the top of the driveway, she was gasping for air. Morgan took Jamie for her second turn but by the third time around, Jamie said she wanted to go by herself. Unfortunately, when she got to the bucket at the bottom of the driveway, she fell and spilled all the water her team had accumulated. But no one even yelled at Jamie; her team came in last, though they didn't seem to mind.

"Next is the food game," Mema said. "Three of our chaperones each have a paper grocery bag, one for each team. There are eight food items in the bags; all the bags contain the same items. When I blow the whistle to start, a team member will reach into the bag and pull out an item. You have to unwrap and completely consume the item before the next person on the team can take one.

"That sounds too easy. There must be a catch on this one, too," Khristian shouted.

"That's right. It sounds easy, but it's not. Wait until you try to quickly drink a whole can of warm soda or chew and swallow 15 marshmallows. Don't worry, though. I didn't put anything gross in the bags. If you have braces and you pull the caramels or the Twizzle sticks, you can throw them back in the bag and select something else. The first team to consume every article in their bag wins."

Mema blew the whistle and the first person on each of the teams grabbed items from the bags. Sarah got eight caramels and had a hard time getting the wrappers off. Khristian pulled out a peanut butter sandwich, no jelly and nothing to wash it down. Talk about dry mouth. Cody came up with jar of baby food, Dutch Apple Treat, which he said tasted good, but didn't come with a spoon. He used two fingers to scoop it out of the jar. Max tried to get the kids to share some goodies with him, but of course they wouldn't.

By the time the food game was over, everyone was mingling nicely.

"It's time for the scavenger hunt," Aunt Liza announced. "Each of the teams will have an adult chaperone. Eric, Team One, AJ's team, John, Team Two, Cody's team, Papa, Team Three, Morgan's team. Each team will have an identical list of twenty items to find. You will have one hour. At the end of an hour, report back here, and the team with the most items will win.

"Please be courteous when you ask people for something. Remember your manners—say please and thank you."

Blah, blah, blah, AJ thought.

The three teams scattered in different directions to begin the scavenger hunt. AJ was glad Uncle Eric, whom she called Uncle Bubbie, was the chaperone for her team, because he was just a big kid at heart. He even let AJ bring Max along with them. Khristian read the list out loud, so the team would know everything they needed to find.

"Is there really such a thing as a 1921 Indian head penny?" he said. They ran to the first house and Sarah rang the doorbell. When Mrs. Johnson came to the door, Sarah asked for an old catalogue. Everyone cheered when Mrs. Johnson brought one out to them.

About twenty minutes later, AJ's team walked up to the hellion children's house. Everyone in the neighborhood said the kids who lived there were little hellions. They received absolutely no discipline or supervision from their parents. They ran wild, threw rocks at kids riding by on their bicycles, harassed AJ and Khristian, and sometimes even stayed outside playing until after eleven o'clock at night. The yard was full of knee-high weeds, broken bicycles, discarded toys, and assorted junk. It was the neighborhood eyesore.

There was a rumor that the dad was recently released from jail. Neighbors said he did time for selling drugs or something. No one knew for sure how many people lived in the house; there were scads of kids, and recently some unsavory characters had been hanging around. Khristian and AJ were afraid of the boys. They were really mean.

"Let's not go here, Uncle Bubbie," AJ said. "They'll probably sic their dog on us." But Uncle Eric and Joe were already knocking on the door, and Max was right behind them. AJ wouldn't even step foot on the property. She used the excuse of taking a picture to stay out on the street.

"Hey, guys, smile!" She snapped the photo just as a mean looking man opened the front door and yelled at them, "Git off my property!"

"No problem," Uncle Eric said. "We didn't mean any harm. We're just having a party, and we're on a scavenger hunt."

"I said git, and take this mangy mutt with you."

Hey, that hurts my feelings, Max thought. Until then, he'd been happily trailing the kids on the scavenger hunt. Suddenly, Max started growling way deep in his throat, and he sounded mega mean—very unMaxlike. Uncle Eric grabbed his collar and tried to pull him away. "Max! Quiet!"

Max pulled loose from Eric's grip and charged the door. The scruffy-looking man slammed it shut just as Max got there. Max jumped against the door, barking and snarling.

The grumpy man yelled through the closed door, "Git that dog outta here!"

Uncle Eric grabbed Max by the collar and dragged him out to the street.

"I've never seen him act like that," Khristian said.

"Neither have I," AJ added.

Uncle Eric said, "Maybe you should take him home before we go to the next house."

But AJ begged, "Please, can we keep him with us? Look, he's quiet now. I don't know what happened. He never acts like that. You know he doesn't." The others joined in, asking to keep Max with them. He was very popular with all of AJ's friends.

Since Uncle Eric knew this wasn't Max's normal behavior, he let him continue on the scavenger hunt with the kids. "But if he does that again," he warned, "You're taking him back home. I don't care if we're at the other end of the subdivision." AJ agreed.

By the time the hour time limit was up, AJ's team had collected only fifteen items. When they got back to the house, both of the other teams were there, and they both had more than fifteen, but the team didn't seem to mind.

The rest of the party was a great success, and the last parents picked up their kids at eleven o'clock. Khristian was spending the night with the Harveys, because he'd wanted to come to the party even though his parents were going out of town.

After both AJ and Khristian showered and got ready for bed, AJ's mom told them they could watch a movie if they were quiet.

"Harry Potter," Khristian yelled.

AJ groaned. "Khristian, I like the movies too, but we've seen every movie in the series at least ten times."

"I know, but I love them," he begged.

Khristian did love the Harry Potter movies. He'd read all the books and had recommended them to AJ. AJ liked Harry Potter too, but she didn't really enjoy watching any movie ten times. But Mema and Papa thought that watching Harry again was a great idea, so began the eleventh viewing.

AJ wasn't paying too much attention to the movie, partly because she was bored and partly because Khristian was speaking all the parts with every character. It was extremely annoying.

Mema said, "Khristian, be quiet—we want to hear the movie." But it didn't do any good. He still kept speaking all the parts.

"Khristian, I'm not kidding. If you don't stop, I'm going to tape your mouth shut," Mema said. Khristian got even louder, so Mems went in the kitchen and got the hundred-mile-an-hour tape and Papa held Khristian down while Mems taped his mouth shut.

"Amy," Mema said. "Get your camera so we can show Khristian's mom how we abuse him when he's here."

This is a lot more fun than watching that movie for the eleventh time, AJ thought.

When everyone finally settled back down to watch the rest of the movie, AJ thought back to how she and Khristian had become BFFs. AJ was five and Khristian was six when they both started bowling in a youth bowling league. For the little kids, the league put "bumpers" in the gutters of the alley. The bumpers kept the bowling ball from going in the gutters so the little kids could hit some pins when they threw the ball.

Now that they were older, they didn't use the bumpers any longer. Back then, AJ's mom and Khristian's mom, the other Amy, sat together every Saturday morning to watch the kids bowl. The two moms became friends, and Khristian and AJ became friends. Khristian's mom home-schooled Khristian, so for socialization activities, Khristian belonged to a drama club, took swimming lessons, and joined the bowling league to meet other kids.

AJ's mom started her in bowling because the YABA youth bowling organization gave out a lot of good scholarships, and since AJ wanted to be a pediatrician when she grew up, scholarship money would make a big difference.

AJ's daydreams were interrupted when Max jumped up and ran to the front door, growling and barking like he had at the hellion children's house earlier.

"Max, be quiet!" Papa said. But Max was charging the door, scratching it and whining.

Papa finally went to the door and grabbed Max's collar. "Hey, boy! Settle down."

"Max is doing that funny growling, deep in his throat again," AJ said.

Papa looked out the window, then opened the front door and looked out.

"It's OK, Max. There's no one there." Papa continued trying to calm Max down, but Max kept pulling away, trying to get out the front door.

"Max, enough. Sit!" Papa commanded, but Max wasn't having any of it. Papa finally closed the door and knelt next to the growling dog, petting him and trying to soothe him.

Amy said, "Maybe there was a cat or something out there. This isn't like Max."

AJ said, "You know what, Papa? Tonight when we were on the scavenger hunt, he did the same thing. We were at the hellion children's house, and he started barking and growling really ferocious, just like now, and he tried to get in their house. Uncle Eric had to drag him away."

"That's because he knows those kids are the devil's spawn," Mema joked.

"That's what Uncle Eric said, too. But, I don't know . . . he's seen those kids before and he's never acted like that. I think it was probably one of those mangy guys that hang around with their dad that he was barking at. Whoever it was, he sure was upset."

"Well, neither those kids nor their dad and his friends are outside our door, so what's got him so upset now?" Papa said.

If he only knew!

"I don't know, but we've missed a lot of the movie, can we rewind it?" Khristian asked.

Everyone groaned and settled back to watch the rest of the movie. Unknown to them, the hellion children's dad and one of his scruffy friends were hiding between the corner of the house and the fence. They dove around the edge of the fence when Papa opened the front door to look outside.

"I am thinking that was way too close. I thought you were saying the peoples are in bed?" Saheb was on his hands and knees peeking around the corner of the house. It took Charles a moment to interpret his singsong method of speaking.

"Well, I never saw no lights on, did you?"

"No, I did not. But I am thinking they must be watching the television set without any lights on. What will we be doing now? We must be getting that camera from Blondie. If they develop that film and anyone recognizes you-know-who, we are all going to be the roast."

"Toast. We'll all be toast. I know, I know. Do you really think your cousin would hurt that little girl just to get her camera?"

"He is a very bad man. Look how he is forcing your family to let us be staying at your house."

"Let's get back ta' my house and try ta' figure somethin' out."

"Maybe we should figure it out before we are going home. We don't want to give him a reason to be hurting the little blondie."

The two men crawled to the edge of the road and stood. They walked to the corner and stopped to talk again.

"Ya know," Charles said, "my girl, Lynn is about the same age as Blondie. What if Lynn could like, go over and pretend to be friends with Blondie. She could steal the camera."

"What a great idea. Now we are having a plan. And if we are having a plan to get the camera, maybe Ali will not be hurting the children." The men returned to the yellow house on the corner.

When Charles was in prison, the man with him, Saheb, was his cellmate. Saheb was born in Pakistan, but his family moved to the United States when he was ten. Saheb wasn't really a bad man, he just wasn't the brightest bulb in the pack. When he and Charles were cellmates, they became friends, of a sort. They spent a lot of time bragging to each other about all the bad things they had done that the police still didn't know about.

Unfortunately, Saheb shared these conversations with his cousin, Ali, who indeed was a very bad man. Ali was a few french fries short of a Happy

Meal too, but he was awfully mean. He currently wanted to be accepted as a member of a terrorist group. But when he approached them, the group laughed at him, so he decided he needed to do something very big and very bad to impress them. Ali threatened to expose Saheb and Charles to the authorities in order to force Charles to allow Ali's gang to stay at his house while they planned their caper. Ali figured that no one would think of looking for them in the home of a typical Florida family.

Back inside the Harvey house, Max sensed the men's departure and settled down. But he also sensed the danger to his humans wasn't totally past, so he stretched out right in front of the front door. No unexpected company would enter the house on his guard.

While the Harveys were sleeping and dreaming, at the yellow house men were scheming and plotting.

"Do you think your girl can get the camera?" Ali asked Charles.

"Well, I gotta admit, there might be a tiny problem with that."

"What might that be?"

"My kid can't stand Blondie. They don't even speak. And my boys have caused quite a bit of fuss over there, you know, startin' fights, snatching bikes and such. I ain't sure any of my kids'd be welcome there."

Ali jumped in, "Well, your girl, she likes to make money, yes? Tell her we will be paying her if she gets the camera for us. That would be the cat's cream."

"Cat's meow," Charles corrected. Then he turned towards the hallway. "Lynn, get your butt in here. I gotta' job fer ya'."

"This better work," Ali snarled. "If it doesn't, I don't care if I have to do away with that whole family, I will get that camera."

The Discovery

The next day, Saturday, AJ and Khristian decided to take Max for a walk when they got home from bowling.

"Maybe you'd better put Max on his leash," Mema said. "The way he's been acting, we don't want to take a chance of him biting anyone or running away."

The kids snapped on Max's leash and left the house. When they passed the hellion children's house, they heard someone calling AJ's name.

"Who's that?" Khristian said.

"I don't believe it. It's Lynn," AJ whispered. I wonder what she wants."

"She probably wants to hold you down so her brothers can cream you," Khristian said. AJ ignored him.

"Hi, Lynn," AJ greeted the other girl. Khristian and AJ walked towards the yellow house to meet Lynn. Max started growling and trying to get on the porch.

"What's wrong with him?" Lynn asked.

"I don't know. He's been acting weird lately," AJ answered.

"Well, our dog, Buddy acts weird all the time. More like he acts stupid all the time. What are you doing later, AJ?"

"Nothing special. Max, stop it." AJ jerked on Max's leash.

"I was wondering if you might want to come over this afternoon for a swim. Our pool's heated, you know. Yours is probably too cold to swim in by now, isn't it?"

"It sure is. Thanks for the offer, but Khristian is spending the weekend with us. His mom and dad are out of town. Max, sit."

"Well," Lynn said, "Khristian can come, too."

"I'll have to ask my mom. Can I call you to tell you if we can come? I don't think I have your phone number."

"It's unlisted. If your mom says OK, just come over about two o'clock. I really hope you can come."

"Bad dog, Max. Sorry, Lynn. OK, we'll go home and ask. I hope we'll see you later."

"Wow, what do you think of that?" AJ asked Khristian when they were out of Lynn's hearing.

"This can't be good. They'll probably try to drown you once they get you in the pool. Are you really going over there?"

"Why not? It's a chance to get to know Lynn. If we get to be friends with Lynn, maybe her brothers won't be so mean to us."

"Dream on, AJ."

They ran home to ask AJ's mom if they could go, but she wasn't too keen on the idea.

"I don't think that's a very good environment for you, AJ. You know the dad just got out of prison."

"I know, but Khristian will be with me." Khristian shook his head no and gestured no way behind AJ's mom's back. When AJ's mom hesitated, AJ added "Can we go, Mom, please?" Khristian gave her a dirty look. "If anything weird happens, we'll come right home. Maybe if we make friends, Lynn will want to go to youth group at church with us tomorrow night. She doesn't seem very happy. I never see her smile." AJ didn't honestly know if she was trying to be nice or just trying to get her mom to let her go. Oh well . . .

"OK, but you can only stay an hour. Come home at three o'clock. If everything goes OK, you can invite Lynn over here later for a cookout with you and Khristian. I'd rather have you kids at our house where I know what's going on."

"Thanks, Mom. As Uncle Eric says, you're the bomb."

"Yeah, thanks a lot," Khristian mumbled under his breath. He didn't want to go to the hellion children's house. Besides always making fun of him, the boys had tried to beat him up several times, but Khristian could run faster than they could.

"Oh, sure," AJ's mom said, "I'm the bomb—when you get your own way."

That afternoon at two o'clock, AJ, Khristian, and Max walked to Lynn's house.

"Max," AJ warned, "You'd better be on your best behavior."

"Like he understands you," Khristian grumped.

"You know what, Khristian?"

"What?"

"If we get to be friends with Lynn, we probably shouldn't call this the hellion children's house anymore."

"Somehow, I don't think that's going to be a problem. I sure hope her brothers aren't home." But to Khristian's dismay, all three boys were home, and worse they were all in the pool.

AJ, Khristian, Lynn, and her three brothers decided to play Marco Polo in the pool. Max sniffed around until he found a spot in the shade to take a nap. He lay under the kitchen window awning, but he couldn't go to sleep, there was too much noise coming through the window. And it was making him very uneasy. Inside the house, Charles and the scruffy men sat at the kitchen table drinking beer, smoking cigarettes, and plotting.

"So far, so good. Now, we need Blondie to invite Lynn to her house so she'll have a chance to get that camera," Ali said. Max sat up to hear better.

Just then Lynn yelled from the pool, "Dad, Martin's cheating, and he hit Khristian."

"What's a matter, izzat Khristian kid a sissy?" Lynn's dad yelled out the window.

Lynn got out of the pool and walked over to the kitchen window. She whispered through the screen, "Look, if you want me to make friends with these kids, you have to call the boys off. They're acting like this is a wrestling match, not a game of Marco Polo. Do you want me to get that camera or not?"

Lynn's dad made the boys come into the house. *Great*, thought Khristian. *Now they'll really hate us.* But he, AJ, and Lynn actually had a pretty good time. At three o'clock, AJ reminded Khristian that they had to go home. Max was standing at the gate, like he knew it was time to leave.

To Lynn, AJ said, "My mom said I could ask you to come over to dinner tonight. We can play basketball or something."

"Sounds good to me. What time?" Lynn asked.

"Come over about five. We probably won't eat until six, but that way we'll have time to shoot some hoops."

When Lynn arrived for dinner, AJ and Khristian were in the driveway playing one on one. Max was lying on the porch watching, and when Lynn arrived, he sat up and watched her every move. The three kids stayed out there until Amy called them in to eat dinner.

After dinner, the kids invited Lynn to watch TV in AJ's room with them. Lynn was ecstatic. This could be her chance to find the camera. Khristian tried to talk the girls into watching a Harry Potter movie again, but they out-voted him for a Hannah Montana episode.

As usual, Max followed the kids into AJ's room, and when Khristian sat on the bed, Max jumped up next to him. AJ and Lynn stretched out on the floor with their backs against the bed. Max seemed to be closely watching Lynn's every move.

A short time later AJ said to Lynn, "There's a good movie coming on soon. What time do you have to go home?"

"No one said when I had to be home. I'm sure I can stay for the movie."

"Great! Khristian, come help me get some snacks. We'll be right back, Lynn."

As soon as they left the room, Lynn took the opportunity to look through AJ's drawers for the camera. She didn't know exactly what it looked like, but she didn't see any cameras lying around. Max still watched her every move. She was just going to open the closet door when AJ and Khristian came back carrying a big bowl of popcorn and some sodas. Lynn jumped away from the door and sat back down on the floor. *I could swear that dog gave me a dirty look*, she thought.

At nine o'clock when the movie was over, AJ's mom said it was time for Lynn to go home. Since it was dark, AJ and Khristian walked her to her house.

"I had a good time, AJ," Lynn said. And she was surprised to realize that she really meant it. But she was worried, too. How was she going to get back into AJ's house to get the camera? She knew her dad wouldn't be happy that she was coming home empty handed. She felt an awful fear in the pit of her stomach thinking about what might happen.

"I had a good time, too," AJ said. "Maybe we can get together tomorrow after church, unless you would like to go to Sunday school with us."

"No, thanks. I'm not much into church. But I'll probably see you when you get home. Come over and maybe we can do something."

When Lynn went into the house, her dad and the three scruffy men who were staying with them were sitting at the kitchen table drinking beers and playing cards as usual. Thinking this was a lucky break, Lynn hurried past the kitchen and went straight to her room and went to bed. It must have been about midnight when she felt someone yank her out of bed by her arm.

"Well, did ja get that camera? Why didn't ya' give it to me when you came in?" Her dad sounded angry, but he looked scared. The other three men didn't look happy either.

"I didn't get it. I only had a minute in her room by myself, and it wasn't enough time."

Saheb's cousin slapped Lynn across the face and she fell back onto her bed crying.

"We told you to get that camera!" he yelled. He drew back his hand to hit her again, but Lynn's dad grabbed his arm.

"Hey, take it easy," Charles said. "She's my kid. I'll handle this. Give her a chance. She'll get it."

"She'd better," Saheb's cousin said. "If she doesn't, I'll go over there and get it myself." Saheb and the other men left the room.

Lynn was rubbing her cheek and tears were streaming down her face. "I will get it, Dad. I will. I just need more time. I'm invited to go back over there tomorrow. You don't want me to get caught, do you? You said it was important that they didn't know it was me taking the camera." Lynn talked fast trying to gain some time to get the camera.

"Aw right. You get another chance. But, Lynn, you gotta get that camera. If we don't get it, I don't know what these guys'll do to us—or to your little friend. They could send me back to jail. They could hurt you or your mom or the boys. We gotta' get that camera. These guys're bad news."

Lynn lay in bed tossing and turning, trying to go back to sleep. She was afraid, and she felt very bad. AJ and her family had been so nice to her, and she wouldn't mind having AJ and Khristian for real friends. But she knew she had to get that camera, she just had to.

The next day, Lynn watched for the Harvey family to come home from church. When she saw their car turning into the subdivision, she decided to walk over to their house to see if she could get invited inside again. The sooner she got that camera, the sooner she could decide if she wanted to be friends with AJ—without trying to steal something from her. It would be nice to have a friend in the neighborhood. She was lonely. Her brothers sure weren't any company.

Lynn couldn't stand her younger brothers; they were wild and they were mean. When her dad was in prison, Lynn's mom had to work two jobs, and Lynn was forced to watch after them. But they never listened to anything she said. She knew that all the neighbors called them the hellion children. In her mind, that's how she thought about her brothers, too.

When Lynn got to the Harveys', AJ invited her into the house. After a few minutes, Lynn found a reason to bring up the Halloween party. She was hoping that the subject of the camera would come up.

AJ said, "I'm sorry you weren't invited to the party Friday night, Lynn. But I didn't know you when we were planning the party. My grandma and grandpa said we could have another one next year. I think they had as much fun as we did."

"That's OK," Lynn said. "Did anyone take pictures? I'd like to see them when you get them developed."

"Yeah, we all took a lot of pictures."

"Do you have your own camera?"

"Yes, I got it for my birthday. It's really easy to use, and it takes great pictures."

Lynn thought, at last. "Can I see your camera? I like taking pictures, too."

"Sure, but you'll have to wait until my Aunt and Uncle get back from their trip. My uncle's camera broke Friday night, so he borrowed mine to take on their vacation."

"How long will they be gone?"

"I think my mom said they would be gone two weeks. When they get home, I'll show you the pictures."

Oh no, Lynn thought. What am I going to do? My dad will be so upset and I'm afraid of what those scruffy men might do. I just want that camera so they'll leave us alone. I need time to think and get that camera.

"AJ, do you and Khristian want to come over for a swim again this afternoon? It's so hot out. I can't believe it's November." Lynn was hoping to postpone a confrontation with her dad and the mean men.

"Are your brothers going to be home?" Khristian asked.

"Yes, but I'll ask my dad to keep them inside. I know you guys don't like them."

"We don't know if we like them or not," AJ said. "They're always so mean; we've never had a chance to get to know them."

Once again, Max accompanied AJ and Khristian to Lynn's house. Khristian was the one who wanted to bring him. He said they might need him for protection.

While the kids swam, Max lay under the kitchen window again. Inside, he could hear Lynn's dad and one of the scruffy men arguing. When he heard AJ's name mentioned, his ears perked up.

"My cousin is wanting that camera. Why is your daughter wasting time? She was at that AJ girl's house again today, but instead of bringing back the camera, she brings back little Blondie, the Pretty Boy, and that mangy dog. You need to be making sure she understands how important it is that we are getting that camera."

"I am. I did. I tol' her again last night after you went to bed. That's why she went over there again today. I don't know why she brought those brats back here."

Saheb said, "Let me be telling you something. If I am having to do it myself, I will be grabbing the little blondie and shaking that camera out of her. I will not be getting beaten by my cousin for not getting the camera."

Max sat up and growled deep in his throat. *Danger! Danger!* He thought. The big dog started pacing around the pool and barking furiously. *Must get away. Must go, now!*

Move, AJ! Move, Khristian! All Max's instincts told him he must protect the children at any cost.

"What's the matter with your dog?" Lynn asked.

"I don't know. He's been acting funny since Friday night. Max! Be quiet!"

But Max continued growling, barking, and pacing around the pool.

Finally, AJ said to Lynn, "I'm sorry, I'm going to have to take him home. I've never seen him act like this. We need to go home anyway. Khristian's mom and dad are supposed to be back by five, and they'll be upset if he's not packed and ready to go home."

AJ and Khristian got out of the pool, put on their shoes, and started home. Max finally quit barking and growling, but he kept tugging on his leash, pulling them away from Lynn's house.

"Thanks a lot, Max. We could have been swimming for another hour. Thanks to you, we have to go home. I hope Lynn isn't mad at me."

Khristian said, "What do you think is the matter with him? That's the way he acted Friday night after the party when we were watching TV. I've never seen him act like that. He's usually so quiet. And he's usually so lazy. Can you believe the way he was running around that pool and barking? I've never seen Max move so fast . . . or so much."

"Beats me. I'm too busy wondering what's going on with Lynn. She's lived here for two years, and as far as I know, she's hated me all that time. When we went to the same school last year, she was so mean to me on the bus; I was scared to get on it every morning. Now, she acts like we're best friends. I don't know why she's being so friendly, but I like it. I hate it when people are mean."

Khristian said, "Let's take the short cut home, through the park."

The park had a small lake and was surrounded by huge live oaks. The lake was home to hundreds of turtles and several small flocks of ducks. The kids walked through there every chance they got.

As they cut across the grass, Khristian took off running and jumped up to touch the lowest branch of a live oak tree. AJ jumped too, but she missed the low hanging branch. She couldn't jump quite as high as Khristian.

"Maybe you need to find out why she's being so nice," said a gruff voice.

AJ ran to catch up with Khristian, "What did you say?"

"I didn't say anything."

"Yes, you did. I was talking about Lynn being so friendly to us, and you made some smart crack."

"No, I didn't. You're hearing things." Khristian ran and jumped up on the bench of a picnic table, ran over the top and down the other side. AJ did the same, like they were playing follow-the-leader.

"Stop, I need to talk to you." Max sat down and scratched his ear.

AJ stopped, too. She sat down on the picnic table bench, but Khristian kept walking.

"Hey! Where are you going?"

"Home, goofus. Come on."

"But you told me to stop."

"I did not."

"Yes, you did."

Khristian ran back to the picnic table. "I did not," he yelled.

AJ started to yell back but was interrupted by the gruff voice again.

"Stop arguing. I need to talk to you."

Both kids looked around to see who was talking to them, but no one was there but Max.

"Stop messing around, Khristian."

"I'm not doing anything. I swear."

"Both of you—sit down and be quiet!" Both kids plopped down on the bench of the picnic table, still looking around for the source of the voice. Max walked over and sat down facing them.

"You both need to listen to me. You're in danger. Especially you, Alyssa."

"Khristian, stop it! This isn't funny anymore." AJ turned ready to poke him in the arm. But when she saw the look on his face, she stopped short. "What?"

"Max," was all Khristian could say.

"What? What about Max?" She knelt down and put her arms around the big dog's neck. "Are you OK, Boy?"

"I'm fine. It's you I'm worried about."

AJ fell back on her rump. "Khristian, stop it. When did you learn to do that?"

Khristian just sat on the bench, wide-eyed, mouth hanging open, shaking his head no, but not saying anything.

"Listen to me. I don't have time to coddle you."

"What does that mean, coddle?" AJ asked.

"It means pamper, indulge, overprotect. Now, be quiet and listen."

To be truthful, there wasn't anything the two kids could do but be quiet and listen. They were, in fact, quite speechless. Max was talking! Max, the dog was talking!

Oh, my Gosh—this is incredible. It's like a fairy tale. No, it's just plain stupid, AJ thought. *My dog is talking. Max is talking.*

And for the first few minutes, neither child heard a word Max said. They were both trying to come to terms with a talking dog. It had to be some kind of a trick.

"You need to stay away from the hellion children's house. Bad men are staying there." Max growled. "They might hurt you."

"Max, are you really talking?" AJ asked.

"Of course I'm talking. What do you think? Khristian's a ventriloquist? Now, be quiet and listen."

"That's exactly what I think. Khristian, I told you to stop!" Again, AJ doubled up her fist to poke Khristian. Again, she was stopped by the look of incredulity on his face.

"Khristian," she shook his arm. "Khristian, you are doing this, aren't you?"

Khristian moved his mouth, but no sounds came out. He shook his head back and forth, but his eyes stared straight ahead at Max.

"No, Khristian is not doing it. Alyssa J. Renae Harvey, listen to me. I need to tell you about the danger." Max turned to look at a family of ducks swimming by. *Can't chase ducks,* he thought. *Have to make the kids believe me.*

"Max, you're talking. Could you always talk?"

"Yes, I have always been able to talk."

"But why didn't you? Why didn't you talk before?"

"I didn't talk . . . I don't talk to humans because, well, think of the chaos it would cause. Just look at the two of you, and kids still believe in magic. Can you imagine how adults would react? They'd probably be doing lab tests on me, or worse, put me on television or something. Make me talk all the time like you humans do. Especially you, AJ."

"Max. I can't believe you're talking. Khristian, Max is talking."

"Maybe you'd better slap his face. He looks like he's in shock," Max said. "Never mind. I'll handle it." Max walked over and nipped Khristian's ankle.

"Ouch! He bit me. I can't believe Max bit me," Khristian said. "That hurt."

"I had to do something. You looked like you were going into shock, and I need to talk to both of you."

"Is this some kind of joke? AJ, do you have a tape recorder somewhere?"

"Yeah, stupid, right here in my swimming suit. No, I don't have a tape recorder. Where would I put it?"

Khristian stopped rubbing his ankle, got off the picnic table bench, knelt down, and got eye to eye with Max. He reached out and touched Max's mouth. "Okay, Max. Say something."

"Your fly is open!"

Khristian jumped up and checked his swimming suit, which of course didn't have a fly.

Max growled a chuckle.

"Not only does he talk, he's got a smart mouth," Khristian said. "Why did you bite me anyway? Look, I'm bleeding. Are you laughing at me? Dogs can't laugh."

"I've always wanted to say that. Now let's get serious for a minute. I have a lot to tell the two of you." Suddenly, Max jumped up and placed his paws on the picnic table bench and whispered.

Can dogs whisper? AJ thought

Max continued, "Act normal until that old lady and her stupid looking excuse for a dog get past. I hope she brought her pooper scooper. That little dog's a menace. Poops more than I do."

One of the neighbors was out walking her Yorkie. The kids waved at her and walked around the picnic table and sat on the other bench, facing the lake instead of the road. Max moved around and sat in front of them, and they waited for the neighbor to pass.

"OK. What's up?" AJ asked. Then she shook her head. *I can't believe I'm talking to my dog.*

"Do you remember when you had the Halloween party, and we were at the hellion children's house on the scavenger hunt?"

AJ answered, "I don't think we should call them that any more. I kind of like Lynn. She's been pretty nice lately."

"She's been O.K.," Khristian added.

"That's because she wants something. When you and Khristian were over there swimming, I was lying under the kitchen window and I could hear them talking inside."

"Ooh," Khristian said. "He even uses good grammar. That will make my mom happy. She hates bad influences."

AJ said, "Does being home-schooled mean everything has to do with education?" AJ asked.

"My mom thinks so," Khristian answered. "School is in session twenty-four hours a day at my house."

AJ rolled her eyes and thought even Max looked disgusted with all this school talk.

Max continued, "I heard Lynn's dad and one of those scruffy men talking in the kitchen. When you kids were on the scavenger hunt Friday night, AJ had her camera along. You must have taken a picture at Lynn's house, and there's something in that picture they don't want anyone to see. Yesterday, they sent Lynn to see if she could get your camera. When the two of you went into the kitchen for snacks last night, she was searching AJ's bedroom—trying to find the camera, I think."

AJ jumped up and put her hands on her hips. "Why, that little sneak. I should have known she wouldn't just all of a sudden start being my friend for no good reason."

"Don't judge her too harshly," Max said. "I think she's afraid of those men staying at her house. When we were over there just now, I heard them talking about how they have to get your camera, no matter what. And I think you're in danger as long as they are trying to get the camera. There's no telling what they might do if they're desperate."

"What should we do, Max?" *I can't believe I'm asking a dog what to do.*

"We should look at those pictures to see if we can figure out what they're trying to hide. When will Uncle Bubbie be back with the camera?"

It sounded so funny to hear Max say Uncle Bubbie.

"We don't have to wait. It's a digital camera, and I downloaded the pictures onto one of the computers at home. We can just go home and print them out. I forgot all about that when Lynn was asking about the pictures."

At that, AJ and Khristian jumped up and started running for home.

"Wait," Max called. The kids turned back to the dog.

"You have to be careful. You cannot, absolutely not, say anything to the adults about me talking. Adults . . . well, adults just wouldn't understand.

They'd make a big deal out of this, call reporters, that kind of stuff. It just can't happen." Max hung his head, "I have broken the Animal Code of Silence. But I felt I had to in order to protect my humans. If this gets out, no other animal will have a thing to do with me. I'll be shunned. If it hadn't been so urgent, if I weren't afraid for your lives, I never would have spoken. Please tell me you understand," Max pleaded.

"I don't see what the big deal is," Khristian said. Max nipped his ankle again.

"OK! OK! I get it. I won't say a word."

"AJ?" Max questioned.

"My lips are sealed."

"That would be a first," Khristian said.

"Right," Max said, "like I'm going to believe Miss Motor Mouth will keep silent."

"I will, Max. I promise. I know I talk a lot. Everyone tells me that. But I know this is important. I'll be quiet. I won't tell a soul." She made the motion of locking her lips and pretending to hand the key to Max.

Since there wasn't anything he could do about it, and since if she did talk no one would believe her anyway, Max accepted AJ's word.

The kids and Max ran home to check out the pictures. But when they got there, Khristian's mom was waiting to pick him up, and AJ's mom said AJ couldn't get on the computer because she had to finish her homework. Just great.

The school week dragged by for both kids. AJ had several tests and a large project due, so there was no time for the camera mystery. She and Khristian didn't talk all week, although they had plans for Khristian to spend the night again the next Friday.

"Has Max been talking to you all week?" Khristian asked as he dumped his sleeping bag on AJ's floor.

"No, he's just acted like a normal dog. I'm beginning to think that we imagined the whole thing."

"No, you didn't imagine anything," Max said as he entered the room. "There just wasn't much we could do during the week, and I didn't want any of the grownups getting suspicious. I know Lynn called you, AJ. You don't plan to go over to the hellion children's house this weekend, do you?"

"Max," AJ started, but Amy stuck her head into the room to say that they were leaving for the movies in fifteen minutes.

After she left, Khristian said, "We need to look at those pictures to see if we can find out what they're afraid of. Then, maybe we can decide if there's really any danger." He was trying to stand in the doorway so no adults could surprise them by coming into the bedroom again.

"There is danger. I have no doubt about that. Do you think I would have blown my cover by talking to the two of you if there really weren't any danger? You two have to get on the computer and print out those photos. These paws don't work very well on computer keys." Max held up a paw, as if he were considering how to type with it.

AJ was thinking, *I didn't know dogs could type. I didn't know dogs could read!*

After the movie, the kids asked if they could look at the pictures from the Halloween party. AJ's mom, Amy helped them set up the photo program. "You can play on the computer for thirty minutes, then it's bedtime." She left and went into her bedroom to watch TV.

"Look, there you are, Harry Potter, glasses and all."

"And there you are. What were you supposed to be, anyway?"

"Very funny. Look, here's the picture I took at Lynn's house. But I don't see anything strange, unless it's these two men standing behind her dad. Maybe that's what it is. Maybe those two guys are criminals."

"Ya think?" Khristian said.

"That doesn't make sense. How would we know if they were criminals? I can't even see their faces very well. Do you know how to enlarge photos? You're the computer geek."

"I am not a geek. Move over and let me try it."

They worked with the photo program until they had an enlargement clearly showing the faces of the two men.

"I don't know how this is going to help us. I've never seen these guys before," AJ complained.

"Let me see," Max said. AJ jumped. She'd forgotten that Max was lying under the computer desk.

While AJ was holding the photo down for Max to look at, Amy came back into the kitchen.

"What are you doing, Alyssa?"

"I'm just showing Max a picture I took of him at the Halloween party. See Max," she said facetiously, "see what a pretty dog you are?"

"If he tells you how much he likes his picture, let me know," Amy chuckled, and left the kitchen again.

"That was too close," Max said. "We have to be more careful."

Khristian was looking at the photo. "What we need is one of those face recognition programs like the cops have in Ybor City."

"I read about that," AJ said. "They used it when the Super Bowl was in Tampa, too. Maybe my Uncle Bubbie can help us. You know, since he's a county deputy. They have wanted posters and stuff, and I think he does something with computers for the sheriff's department."

"Yeah," Khristian said, "we'll just tell him that Max told us we're in danger because we took a picture of these two guys. That'll go over real big. Max would probably bite me on the other ankle."

"Then how are we going to find out who they are? Do you have any other ideas, wise guy?"

"Well, I have one, but I don't know if it will work. Why don't you invite Lynn to go on the mystery retreat with the youth group next weekend? We can try to become friends with her, and maybe she'll tell us what's going on. Maybe she's afraid of her dad and needs our help. You know how they always tell us at youth group that we need to reach out to other kids; especially kids we think might be in trouble."

"I don't think that's such a great idea," Max interrupted. "That would mean spending more time with her, either here or at her house. It would be dangerous."

"What else are we going to do, Max? Why don't we go over there tomorrow? If you're worried, you can go with us again. Since no one knows you can talk, you can try to overhear more conversations and maybe you can find out what's going on?"

"Yeah, that's a good idea," Khristian added, "only this time, you can't start barking and growling and acting like an idiot. You'll give us away."

"I beg your pardon. I do not act like an idiot, neither now nor have I ever. I was trying to get your attention and get you out of there. As for your idea, I suppose you would be safe enough, especially since you told them Uncle Bubbie has your camera and he won't be back for another week. OK, let's try going over to Lynn's house tomorrow to see if we can learn anything else. And you can go ahead and invite Lynn to the retreat next weekend. I just wish I could come to keep an eye on all of you."

"Thanks for your permission, Max. Who put you in charge, anyway?"

"Let's have a little respect for your elders."

"What do you mean, elders? We got you when I was three years old. Now I'm eleven and you're eight. You need to show me some respect," AJ said.

"I'm eight in human years, but that's fifty-six in dog years."

"Eek! You're as old as Mema. Poor old Max! Do you want a cane?"

AJ's mom interrupted when she came into the kitchen, "I told you kids only 30 minutes on the computer. It's time to go to bed. Khristian, do you have to go home after bowling tomorrow, or can you hang around with AJ tomorrow afternoon? I have some errands I need to do, and you could keep her company."

"I don't know what my mom's got planned, but I'd like to stay here. We can ask her when she comes to watch us bowl in the morning."

"OK. Why don't you let me ask her? She's more likely to say yes if I ask."

"Thanks, Miss Amy."

Khristian got his duffel bag and went into the bathroom to change into his PJs. AJ closed her bedroom door and started to change her clothes.

She quickly opened it again, pointed toward the hallway and said, "Max, get out of here!"

"Why? I'm not doing anything."

"Because I need to change clothes."

"So, go ahead."

"Not in front of you. You're a boy!"

"I've seen you change clothes a million times. What's your problem?"

"That was before I knew how human you are. Get out." AJ pushed Max's rump through the door and shut it before he could come back in.

The next morning when the kids were getting dressed to go bowling, AJ and Khristian weren't getting along too well.

"Khristian, you need to get out of the bathroom," AJ yelled.

"I'll be out in a minute," Khristian snapped.

Amy came out of her bedroom. "What's the matter? Why are you yelling at Khristian?"

"He's been in the bathroom for forty-five minutes." AJ doubled up her fist and pounded on the door. "I still have to take a shower, wash my hair, and get dressed." She pounded on the door again. "Why does he always have to take so long?" She banged the door once again for emphasis.

"I can't believe he's been in there for forty-five minutes," Amy said.

"Well, he has! That's because his hair has to be perfect for Meg—an," AJ sang. "His hair's only two inches long. How can it take so long to comb it? I'll tell you how it takes so long. First he has to 'gel' it. Then he makes every spike stick up just so . . ."

"Just use my bathroom," Amy interrupted. "It's not worth fighting over."

"I'd rather use your bathroom anyway. The toilet in this one's making that goblin sound again."

"Have you told Papa so he can fix it?"

"I keep forgetting. Do you think there's something alive in there?"

"Just get ready to leave, Alyssa."

Later that morning at bowling, Khristian's mom, the other Amy, said he could stay at the Harveys' until three-thirty. After bowling, AJ, Khristian, and Max walked over to Lynn's house. She was sitting on the front porch.

"Hey, guys! What are you doing?"

"Not much. We came over to invite you on the mystery retreat for our church youth group. We leave next Friday night, and we get home Sunday afternoon."

"Where are you going?"

"We don't know. That's the mystery. But all the older kids said they always have a blast. All you need is a sleeping bag and some spending money. Do you want to come?"

"I don't know. I'll have to ask. When would I need to let you know?"

"We have to tell the leaders by Wednesday night. I hope you can come. I think we'll have a lot of fun."

"When does your Uncle get back so I can see the pictures of your Halloween party?" Lynn asked.

"Oh, they should be home some time Friday. I hope he gets home before we leave so I can take my camera with me." AJ winked at Khristian, who thought she was being way too obvious.

Another week before I can get that camera. My dad's going to kill me. What will those scruffy men do? Lynn's thoughts were interrupted by AJ.

"Do you want to do something this afternoon?" she asked. "Khristian and I aren't doing anything right now."

Lynn brought out a Monopoly game, and the three of them played at a table near the pool.

"My Aunt Liza would love to be here—she loves Monopoly. She has at least ten sets. She has NASCAR Monopoly, Scooby Doo Monopoly, Disney Monopoly, National Parks Monopoly, South Tampa Monopoly, she even had a chocolate Monopoly until her dog ate it . . . ," AJ went on and on.

Max again took a position under the open kitchen window. The men were once again in the kitchen drinking beer and playing cards. Max hoped he would hear something to help solve the mystery. Mystery retreat, neighborhood mystery men; that was one mystery too many for Max's liking.

At three-fifteen AJ and Khristian left so they could be at AJ's house when Khristian's mom came to pick him up. As soon as they were out of earshot of the hellion children's house, they began pelting Max with questions.

"Max, did you hear anything?"

"What did they say? Come on—no one's around. You can talk to us."

"When will you two learn that I only talk when I have something to say? I didn't hear anything except a lot of swearing and belching. Those scruffy men have dreadful manners."

Meanwhile, at Lynn's house, when AJ and Khristian left, Lynn's dad called her into the kitchen.

"Well? When are you gonna get that camera?"

"Dad, I told you that her uncle took it with him on vacation. He's supposed to be home by this weekend. Those kids invited me to go on a trip with their church youth group. We would leave Friday night and be back Sunday. Can I go?"

"I used to go to church when I was a kid," Charles reminisced. Then he snapped, "You ain't goin' on no trip with no church group. What are ya' thinkin? We gotta get that camera. We don't have no time for no church trips."

"Dad, think about it. I figure if AJ's uncle is home by the time we leave Friday, AJ will take her camera with her on the trip. That would give me all weekend to get it. There'll be a whole bunch of kids on the trip, and no one will know that I was the one who took it."

"All right. But this is yer last chance. If ya don't get that camera this weekend, I don't know what's gonna happen to us. Lynn, honey, these guys mean business, and they want that camera. I know I ain't the best dad in the world, but I love you kids and yer mom, and I don't want nothin' to happen to ya." Charles put his arms around Lynn and hugged her. He never did that. She was so surprised, she started crying.

"Dad, I will get that camera for you. I promise. Dad, why are you letting these guys stay here? Can't you make them leave?"

"I don't want nothin' more than to have 'em gone. But, well, you know I done some bad things in the past?"

"What's that have to do with them being here?"

"That Saheb, well, he was my cellmate when I was in prison. I told him some of the things I done, and he told his cousin, Ali. Now Ali says he'll turn me in ta the cops if I don't help 'em."

"Oh, Dad. What have you gotten us into?"

By the time AJ and Khristian arrived back at the Harveys' house, Lynn was already calling to say that she would be going on the mystery retreat with them the next Friday. When AJ got off the phone, she and Khristian took Max into her room and closed the door.

"Max, that was Lynn who called. She's going on the trip with us next weekend."

"I'm still not so sure this is a good idea," Max said. "I'm worried about what might happen to you kids without me there to watch out for you."

"Max, we'll be fine," AJ said. "The scruffy men aren't going on the trip, and Khristian and I will keep a close eye on Lynn. That is if Khristian can keep his eyes off Meg—an."

"What's that supposed to mean?" Khristian asked.

"Just that you've got a huge crush on Megan. You sure are girl-crazy all of a sudden."

"I am not. Anyway, what about you and Co—dy? AJ and Cody, sitting in a tree . . ."

"Knock it off," Max yelled.

"Sorry, Max. Where were we?"

"We were talking about what is going to happen on this trip without me there to keep you two in line."

"I sure wish we knew why they want my camera so bad. I mean, I know they want the pictures, but why?"

"Yeah," Khristian added, "we've looked at those pictures over and over again, and we don't see anything in them they could want. I know we talked about this before, but do you think those two guys in the picture are wanted by the cops?"

Max said, "I would bet my next Milk Bone that those two men are wanted."

"Yeah, right. Like you'd ever give up one of your Milk Bones. Khristian, the last time Uncle Bubbie brought his two dogs, Mick and Misha, over I thought Max and Mick were going to get into a fight over a Milk Bone."

"It wasn't Mick, it was Misha. German shepherds have rotten attitudes. Think they own the world. She'd already eaten her treat, and she thought she'd just have mine, too," Max added indignantly. "Now, back to our mystery. Isn't there some kind of web site on the computer where they put pictures of criminals?"

"Probably. But I wouldn't know where to begin looking. And even if I did, my mom's got my Internet access set so that I can only go on web sites she approves of, so I can't just go out and search the web. We need more information," AJ said.

"I wish we could get Lynn on our side. If she would just talk to us, tell us what's going on, we might be able to figure this out. We need to get her to trust us," Khristian said. "That's the only way we'll be able to help her."

"Even if she trusts you, I don't think she'll tell you what's going on. From everything I've heard, I think she's too afraid of her father; and she's terrified of those scruffy men," Max said.

Just then Amy stuck her head in AJ's room, "Who are you two talking to?"

"Each other. Why?" Khristian asked.

"I thought I heard someone else." Amy reached down and gave Max a pat on the head. "Hey Max! Are you having a conversation with the kids?" Max answered her with doggie kisses.

"Must have been the TV," AJ said.

Amy shrugged, "Mr. K, your mom's here. Do you have all your stuff together?"

After she left the room Max said, "We've got to be more careful. She almost caught us talking that time."

"Stop being a worry wart, Max. She'd never believe we were talking to you, I mean that you were talking, I mean, oh never mind."

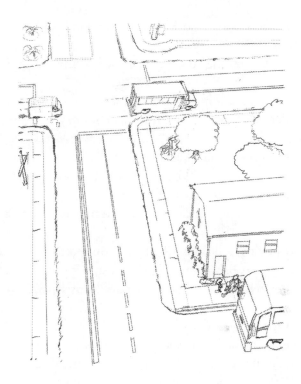

Retreat—Don't Run

The following week was crammed with school, homework, choir, youth group, and chores. There was no time to work on solving the mystery. On Friday night while AJ was packing for the retreat, Max came in to watch.

"I'm still not sure this is a good idea," he said.

"Max, we'll be fine. There are going to be 45 kids and 7 chaperones. What can happen?"

"I don't even want to imagine. Promise me one thing. If anything strange happens, you'll go to one of the adults and tell them."

"Tell them what? My dog's worried and I think something weird is going on? Max, Lynn won't be able to do anything with all those people around. Stop worrying."

Khristian's mom, Amy, and Khristian came into AJ's room. "Are you all packed and ready to go?" she asked AJ.

"Yep, I'm just rolling up my pillow in my sleeping bag," AJ answered.

Amy gave Khristian a hug. "You kids have a great time. I'm going to go meet your dad for dinner now. I'll see you Sunday." Amy gave AJ a hug too, and left the room.

"OK, kids. Tonight you're leaving for the mystery retreat. I want you both to promise me that you'll be very careful. I won't be there to watch over you." Max was very worried.

"We know, we know, Max, and we promise we'll be careful, right, Khristian?"

"Yeah, we'll be careful, Max." Khristian turned to AJ, "Should we tell him about tomorrow, or wait and let it be a surprise?"

"We'd better tell him so he can prepare himself," AJ said. *Was Max looking alarmed?*

"What? What are you two talking about? Prepare myself for what?"

"Max, I've got some bad news for you."

"What? Does it have to do with the scruffy men?" Max asked. Then he growled, "Khristian, what are you laughing about?"

AJ knelt in front of Max and put her arm around the big dog's neck, "No, it's not the scruffy men. Max, I'm afraid it's the big 'G'."

"Grooming," Max yelled, "Oh, no! Anything but that."

"I'm afraid so. Mema made an appointment for tomorrow morning. You're going to a new grooming place called Fluffy Cuts."

"Fluffy Cuts?" Max butted Khristian with his head. "Khristian, stop laughing. Fluffy Cuts? It sounds like some sissy dog place. AJ, tell Mema not to let them put a bow in my hair, please? Khristian, I'm going to bite you again if you don't stop laughing."

"Oh, it's OK for you to tell me my fly is open and laugh at me, but I'm not allowed to laugh at you or you'll bite me? How would you like it if I bit you?"

"OK you two, stop it. We've got more important things to worry about," AJ said.

"Easy for you to say," muttered Max.

Max would have been even more upset, indeed, if he knew what was going on at the hellion children's house.

Saheb and Charles were on the patio. Saheb said, "I am not having a good feeling about the chances of your girl getting the camera."

"What choice've we got? She's gonna be with Blondie and those other kids all weekend. She'll come through for us."

"Well, I am not counting on that. Go and get your van ready to drive."

"You know I don't got a driver's license."

"I am thinking it does not matter. We are going to be following those children on this mystery retreat. Then, when they are all sleeping, we will slide into the camp and get the camera ourselves."

"We'll slip into the camp."

"That is what I said. Why must you always be correcting my English?"

"Whatever. Sneakin' inta the camp sounds pretty dangerous to me."

"No, what is dangerous is what will happen to us if we do not get the camera. My cousin, Ali is getting very much anxious. You do not want to see what he is like when he is angry. The big date is still two months away. If anyone recognizes him in those pictures, and the police come smelling around, it will ruin everything he is trying to do. He is a very mean man when he is not getting his way."

"When the police come sniffing around, not smelling."

"There, you are doing it again. I am thinking that my English is very good. Yet, you are correcting me all the time."

The argument was interrupted by the doorbell. When Charles opened the door, it was AJ, coming to pick up Lynn for the retreat. Lynn grabbed her sleeping bag, overnight bag, and AJ's arm. "Come on, let's go," and she pushed AJ back out the door.

Charles and Saheb waited ten minutes before they drove to the church to follow the kids' bus.

"Park in that empty lot across the street," Saheb said. "Then we can see the bus when it leaves." Car after car full of kids arrived at the church annex. The kids and their parents went into the fellowship hall for their final instructions.

Sooner than Charles and Saheb thought possible, they saw the bus pull out from the parking lot behind the church.

"Hey, there they are going. Hurry up. Do not be losing them."

"There's not much chance of that," Charles muttered. "That bus is huge, plus it's white and it has the name of the church painted on the side in big red letters. How can we lose it?"

"Why are they driving so slowly?" Saheb complained.

"Who knows? It looks like they got some old geezer driving."

"Who? You were not telling me that you are knowing the driver of the bus, this geezer."

"It's just a sayin'—never mind. Just keep your eyes on the bus. And watch out for cops. Remember, I don't got no driver's license."

The men didn't realize that there were two church groups going on bus trips that night, and they were following the wrong bus. The bus they were following was full of senior citizens going to a Mel Torme concert at Ruth Eckerd Hall. The bus with the kids was still back at the church.

The vehicles turned off of Highland Street onto the eastbound lanes of East Bay Drive. Just as they passed the intersection of Keene and East Bay, they heard a siren.

Charles looked in the rear view mirror and saw a police cruiser about two blocks behind him and closing rapidly. "I knew it. I just knew it. What should I do? Should I pullover? Should I run? If I run and they catch me, it's all over. If I stop it's all over. I knew we shouldn't try this."

Soon the squad car was right behind Charles, who was sweating and swearing under his breath. Suddenly, the squad car pulled around him and continued up East Bay Drive. Charles was shaking so badly that he had to pull over and park the van.

Saheb was yelling at him, "Go, go. We must not be losing that bus. Move it! Move it! You must push yourself together. Let's go!"

"Pull myself together, not push," Charles automatically corrected as he pulled back into traffic.

The bus was about two lights ahead of the van, but the men could still see it plainly because it was so big, so white, and moving so slowly that all the normal traffic was passing the bus. The van moved in fits and spurts through the stream of traffic, trying to keep the bus in sight yet stay far enough back so they wouldn't be noticed.

When the bus reached 49th street, it turned north, to cross the 49th Street Bridge. The van, lagging behind a bit too far, got stopped at the traffic light when some tourist stopped for a yellow light.

Saheb was yelling again. "What is that stupid tourist doing? Even I know that drivers are not stopping for yellow lights in Florida. It must be an ice bird."

"Snow bird," Charles corrected. "We call them snow birds, 'cause they migrate down here when it snows up north—just like the birds."

The light finally turned green, and Charles floored the accelerator, squealing tires and passing the tourist car on the on-ramp to the bridge. He cut off two other cars as the van merged into the bridge traffic, trying to catch the bus.

"You are going to be getting us killed!" Saheb yelled.

"We've got to catch that bus. They could be goin' anywhere from here. If we don't catch 'em on the bridge, we'll never find 'em."

As the van reached the north end of the bridge, the men saw the bus crossing the intersection, still traveling north. Like so many streets, roads, and highways in Florida, the road changed names as it passed the intersection. On the north side of the Gulf-to-Bay Boulevard intersection, it became McMullen-Booth Road.

Charles' bad luck continued, and he again had to stop for a traffic light, an actual red one this time.

When the light finally turned green, the van squealed off again to catch the bus. Charles was going so fast, he drove right past the bus, which was sitting in the right hand turn lane, waiting to enter the Ruth Eckerd Hall parking lot. Just as the van pulled even with the bus, Saheb looked to the right and spotted it. "Look! The bus—it's turning in here."

"For cryin' out loud," Charles yelled, "now I gotta go to the next light and turn around and come back. It's a good thing you spotted 'em. I coulda' been all the way to Tarpon Springs before we figured out we missed 'em. What the heck are they taking a bunch of kids to Ruth Eckerd Hall for? Are they havin' some rock concert or something?"

Charles sped to the next light, slammed on his breaks, and squealed his tires making a U-turn to get back to Ruth Eckerd Hall. But once they arrived, the bus was nowhere in sight. The men drove through two parking lots before they spotted the bus. Charles attempted to drive over some traffic cones blocking the entrance to that parking area, but one of the parking attendants ran out in front of the van, and he had to slam on his breaks.

A man with a face like a bulldog tapped a flashlight as big as a baseball bat on Charles' side window. Charles slowly cranked the window down.

"What do you think you're doing? Can't you see those traffic cones? You can't turn in here. This lot is full. Turn around."

"We need 'ta get in this lot," Charles said. "We got friends parked in this lot."

"Well, I just told you, the lot's full. Now back up and head toward the back of the building. The overflow parking is back there."

Charles rolled up his window. "Great! Just great. Look over there. They're gettin offa the bus. Man, those kids ain't gonna have no fun. Look how old those chaperones are. Where are the kids, anyway? I wonder if they let 'em off back at the front door?"

Mr. Bulldog tapped his flashlight on Charles' window again. "I said move it, Bud. Now!"

By the time Charles and Saheb found a parking place in the overflow lot and walked back to the lot where the church bus was, it was empty. Even the driver was gone.

"Well, I guess we're gonna have ta' go inside. Who knows? Maybe it'll be easier here. There's more people. And if we see Blondie with the camera, we can grab it and run. They might not even notice us in the crowd."

The men walked around the building to the box office. "I'm sorry. We're sold out," the ticket agent told them.

"Hey, we'll take anything. How 'bout standing-room-only tickets? You got any of those?" Charles pleaded. But it was no use. The concert was sold out. The men stood on the sidewalk at the corner of the building trying to decide what to do.

"Psst!"

"Who said that?"

"I did." A man in dark jeans and a t-shirt was standing out of sight of the box office. "You guys want tickets?"

"Yes," Saheb said, "we would be liking some tickets. Do you have some?"

"Yeah, but it'll cost you."

"And how much would these tickets be costing," Saheb said.

"Sixty bucks each."

"Sixty bucks? That's highway robbery," Charles said. But Saheb removed a large roll of twenty-dollar bills from his pocket and peeled off six of them.

Charles and Saheb grabbed the tickets and rushed inside.

"We are going to need a plan," Saheb said. "I am thinking that we should be split up. We will be meeting back here in twenty minutes. Once we are finding Blondie, we will wait for the intermission. Then, when she is in a big crowd of people, we will be grabbing the camera and skoot-paddling out of here."

"That's skedaddling," Charles said. "Ya' gotta stop butcherin' the English language. All right, I'll see ya back here in twenty minutes."

Charles searched the main floor and Saheb climbed to the mezzanine. The men walked slowly up and down the aisles looking for the group of kids from the church, but neither man could find them. When they met back in the lobby, they were puzzled.

"I am wondering why they would bring children to hear this man sing. He is singing songs older than my mother," Saheb said.

"Yeah. I don't get it either," Charles answered. "Did ja have any luck?"

"No. And the interruption is in five minutes."

"Intermission. It's called intermission. Now what're we gonna do?"

"Let us go and wait by the exit. When the concert is being over, they will come out of the doors and we will be seeing them. I still am not believing it is costing sixty dollars for a person to hear this old man, this spooner, sing. What must they be thinking?"

"That's crooner—they call him a crooner," Charles corrected.

The men stationed themselves next to the main exits. When the concert was over, they examined every single face, but didn't see any of the kids from the church.

"I am seeing nothing but old people. Where are the children? Do you think they are waiting in the hobby for the bus to pick them up?

"It's lobby. Oh, never mind. You'll never get it."

They checked back inside the lobby, but still didn't see any of the kids, and the auditorium was empty except for two tired janitors sweeping the floors.

"This is useless. Let's go and be waiting by the bus," Saheb said.

But as they were walking out the front doors, they saw the white bus. It was pulling out of the parking lot onto McMullen-Booth Road.

"How did they get by us?" Sahib screamed. "There must be a back door." The men ran to the van, but it was no use. By the time they reached the overflow parking lot and retrieved the van, the bus was out of sight.

"Well, Charles, I am hoping your girl will be having better luck than we have had. I am hoping she will be coming home with little Blondie's camera, or you and I may be having our throats sliced by my cousin and his friend."

"Well, we ain't got no choice but to go home and wait for em to get back on Sunday," Charles said. It was a silent ride back to the hellion children's house.

The bus full of senior citizens who went to Ruth Eckerd Hall to see the Mel Torme concert had a wonderful time. And the bus filled with the children going on the mystery retreat was halfway to the Disney campground in Orlando.

The children's bus was a cacophony of noises. Kids were talking, laughing, singing, playing travel games, and just plain having a great time. In addition to promoting spiritual growth, Robby and Amanda, the young couple in charge of leading the youth group, worked hard to make every outing fun for the kids.

The entire center of the bus was filled with AJ and Khristian and their close circle of friends. AJ sat with Lynn, and Khristian and Cody sat directly behind them. Across the aisle from AJ and Lynn were Justine and her twin brother Joe, and behind them Sara and Megan, Khristian's girlfriend. More friends, Morgan and Amy, sat in front of AJ and Lynn.

Khristian and AJ had spoken with each of their friends and asked them to help Lynn feel at home and help her to have a good time on the retreat. Currently, the kids were trying to guess where the bus was headed. It wasn't too hard to determine that their destination was Orlando, since they were traveling east on I-4.

When the bus reached Wilderness campground in Orlando, Robby and Amanda announced that the next day would be spent at Disney World, and Saturday evening they would continue to the east coast. Saturday night they would camp at Daytona Beach where the kids would have an opportunity to take surfing lessons on Sunday before heading back home. Cheers and whistles raised the noise level even higher.

Before bedtime that night, the group gathered for devotions. Robby shared about the love of God: how He loves each one of us so much that he sent his Son, Jesus so that we could accept salvation, be forgiven of our sins, and be reconciled to God.

I wonder what Lynn thinks of these devotions, AJ thought. She sneaked a glance at Lynn and saw tears in her eyes. AJ sent up a silent prayer. *Thank you, Father God. I know you have touched Lynn's heart. Help us all to show her your love.*

After the devotion, there was a silence rule. The kids were to go back to their tents and go to bed without speaking. They were each to think about what the devotion meant to them, and what God was speaking into their hearts personally. For once, AJ was glad that she wasn't allowed to say anything. She was wise enough to know that the Holy Spirit was much more capable of speaking to hearts than she was, even though she really did love to talk.

The next morning, Lynn pulled AJ aside after breakfast. "AJ, I really need to talk to you and Khristian, but I don't want anyone else to hear."

"Gee, Lynn, look at this schedule I just picked up from Amanda. It's like every minute is scheduled for some activity. These retreats are so busy, I don't know if we'll find time for just the three of us to get together. Khristian and I really want to talk to you, too. Can it wait until we get home tomorrow night?"

"I guess it will have to. It's really important, though."

Back home in Largo, Mema and Papa were getting Max ready to go to the new grooming place. Max was hiding in Amy's shower.

"Come on, Max. You can't hide from me. I know all your hiding places," Mema said as she snapped on his leash. "I think you'll like this new place. The people there are very nice."

I love to ride in the van, Max thought. *It's too bad it has to be a trip for grooming. I'd much rather go to Tastee Freeze. They always give me a doggie cone. Maybe we'll go to Tastee Freeze after the groomers.*

Papa pulled into the lot of a small, neat looking building. "Here we are, Max. You're going to love this," Mema said.

I hope AJ remembered to tell Mema not to let them put a bow in my hair.

"And don't worry. I'll tell them not to put a bow in your hair."

AJ rocks, Max thought.

Inside the building, another couple was waiting with the most beautiful dog Max had ever seen.

I think I'm in love, Max thought. "Hi, Gorgeous," Max communicated in dog language.

"Gee," Mema said, "I thought Max was going to give us a hard time. He usually doesn't like being groomed, and he tries to leave when we do. He must really like this new place."

"It's more likely that he likes that pretty golden retriever," Papa said. "Max looks smitten. Don't forget to tell them not to put a bow in his hair."

Yeah, Papa. You rock, too!

Mema and Papa signed Max in and left to have breakfast while he was being groomed. When they returned to pick him up, Max was looking quite spiffy indeed. He was fluffy clean, his coat was trimmed, and he wore a sporty new handkerchief tied around his neck. Max practically pranced out to the van.

I'm cool! I'm the bomb. If Goldy could only see me now, she'd drop that Irish setter like a bad bone.

In Orlando, the kids were having a great time at Disney World. AJ, Lynn, Megan, and Sarah were standing in line for a second ride on Splash Mountain. Khristian and Cody ran up to the girls, "Hey! We rode Space Mountain three times. You girls are soaked. How'd you get so wet?"

"This is our second time on Splash Mountain. It's a good thing its warm today or we'd be freezing."

"You're gonna be freezing in about an hour. The temperature drops fast this time of the year when the sun sets."

"Then you can have an excuse to keep Megan warm," AJ joked.

"No purpling! No purpling!" Sarah shouted, and they all laughed. Robby and Amanda said boys were blue and girls were pink, and they didn't want those two colors mixing to make purple.

That night on the bus as they were traveling to Daytona Beach, Lynn seemed very happy. It was the only time AJ could ever remember seeing her so animated.

"Man, Khristian really got soaked on Splash Mountain," she said.

"He sure did. I don't think he minded getting wet. He was just upset that all his hair gel got washed out." AJ laughed.

Khristian reached over the seat and yanked on AJ's ponytail. "I heard that," he said. "Don't make fun of me when I'm freezing to death."

The kids had packed all their belongings and loaded them onto the bus luggage bin before they went to the park, so Khristian didn't have anything dry to put on.

"I have my jacket in my back pack. Do you want to use it?" Sarah asked. AJ loved Sarah. She had red hair and freckles and wore tiny little black-framed reading glasses. Sarah was always in a good mood.

"That would be great," was Khristian's shivery reply. "I'm freezing. My teeth are chattering and I can't stop." Everyone burst out laughing at the sound he made with his teeth.

"You kids all seem to get along so well," Lynn said to AJ. "And everyone is always so helpful to everyone else. Today, I wasn't thinking, and I left most of my money in my overnight bag. Sarah bought me lunch and said I could pay her back tomorrow, and Allie bought me a drink this afternoon."

"That's why I love belonging to this youth group so much," AJ said. "We try to practice the Christian principles that Robby and Amanda are teaching us. One of the ways we do that is on missions trips."

"What's a mission trip?" Lynn asked. "Have you been on one?"

"Not yet. You have to be in seventh grade. Last summer the junior high kids went to a small church in central Florida, in Wimauma. They helped build a playground for migrant workers' children. It was hard work, but they all said they had fun, too."

"Did they get paid for doing it?"

"No. They did it to help the church in Wimauma. A lot of workers who come to Florida from Mexico to work in the orchards or on farms leave their kids in that church day care center. That's a really small church, and they don't have much money. Our church is huge, we have over 4,000 members. We're lucky to have a lot of people who are willing to donate money to help others, like that little church."

"I don't get it," Lynn said.

"You will," AJ answered. *You will.*

On the bus ride back the next day, Lynn was very quiet. *How am I going to tell AJ and Khristian about the scruffy men? Hey, AJ, I was sent to your house to steal the film out of your camera. That should go over great. I don't want to get my dad in trouble, but I don't want my new friends hurt. I wish I could get that film and put an end to this mess. I have to figure out what I'm going to say by the time we get back to the church.*

However, when the bus arrived back at the church, the parents were already waiting to take their kids home. Robby and Amanda had called one of the moms as the bus passed through Tampa, and she had called the other parents to let them know the kids would be home shortly.

"Come on, Lynn. There's my mom." AJ grabbed her sleeping bag and suitcase and headed for the Jeep.

Lynn grabbed her arm, "When are we going to talk?"

"How about later tonight? Aren't you anxious to get home?"

Not really, Lynn thought. She gathered her stuff and shuffled over to the Jeep.

"Guess what?" Amy said. "Never mind, I can't wait for you to guess. We've got tickets to the Florida—Florida State game."

"Wow! How did we get those?" AJ asked.

"Well, Outback Steakhouse has a big block of tickets, but now, there are big doings at the Outback corporate office that day, and they won't be using all of their tickets. They called Aunt Liza to see if she wanted them.

"My Aunt Liza worked her way through college as a nanny for some of the people who started Outback Steakhouse," AJ explained to Lynn. "Sometimes Liza gets tickets to sporting events that the Outback corporate office isn't using. We got to sit in the Outback Suite for several Devil Rays baseball games. Last year we had great tickets for the Outback Bowl. My mom wanted to go because she loves the Gators, and they played in the Outback Bowl last year. Mom even got to go down on the field by the players. And now we're going to the Florida—Florida State game. Yippee!"

"AJ, enough," Amy said. "Stop and take a breath."

"I do love the Gators," Amy explained to Lynn. "And AJ plans to attend the University of Florida when she's ready for college. My brother Eric is a die-hard Seminole fan. Now the whole family gets to go to the Gator-Seminole game. You probably think we're being silly, but this is probably the biggest college football game of the year in Florida, even bigger than the Gator-Hurricane game. Do you like football, Lynn?"

"How many tickets do we have?" AJ interrupted. "Do you think we'll be able to take Khristian and Lynn?"

"I'm not sure. I've already invited Khristian's family. We're still waiting to hear back on the exact number of tickets, though."

"Where's the game going to be?" Lynn asked.

Amy answered, "At the Swamp. That's the nickname for the Gators home field. Aren't you excited, AJ?"

"Excited isn't the word for it. I'll get to see my future college. I can't wait."

AJ and her mom rattled on with talk about the game and the family rivalry. But Lynn didn't pay attention, she just zoned out of the conversation. *What's going to happen to me? I didn't get the film from the Halloween party. Are those men going to hurt my dad?*

When they dropped Lynn off at home, AJ said, "Lynn, if we have enough tickets, would you like to go to the game with us?"

"What did you say?"

"I said, if we have enough tickets, do you want to go to the game with us? Mom said if we have enough tickets, I can invite you."

Lynn was so shocked that she didn't know what to say.

"Gee, I'd love to, AJ. But I'll understand if you don't have enough tickets. Can we get together later? I'd still like to talk to you."

Amy interrupted, "I'm sorry, but AJ won't be able to get together tonight, Lynn. She has homework to finish and things she needs to do to get ready for school tomorrow. Why don't you come over and have dinner with us one night this week. AJ can call you tomorrow to let you know when."

AJ helped Lynn carry her stuff up to the porch, and the girls said good-bye.

"I know you wanted to talk to Khristian and me about something, and I'm sorry we didn't have the chance. When you come over for dinner, I'll invite Khristian to come too, and we can talk then."

Lynn had tears in her eyes. "AJ, I really need to talk to you. Are you sure you can't come over later?"

"I'm sure. When I've been gone all weekend, my mom never lets me go anywhere as soon as I get home. What's the matter? Didn't you have a good time at the retreat?"

"I had a great time," Lynn answered. "It's just that it's so important that I talk to you."

"Lynn," Amy called from the car, "would you like to go to youth group with AJ on Wednesday? If you would, you can have dinner with us Wednesday night. If you'd like to go, ask your parents and let us know."

"Thanks, Miss Amy," Lynn called. "I'll call you later, AJ." Lynn dragged her bags into her house.

At home, Mema gave AJ a big hug, "Hey, Sweetie. Tell us all about your trip."

"I need a hug, too," Papa said.

It was another hour before AJ and Max had a chance to go into AJ's room and discuss the retreat.

"Max, you look great. I love that kerchief. I did what you asked, and I told Mema not to let them put a bow in your hair. Have you been wearing that kerchief since you got groomed yesterday?'

"No. Papa took it off last night so it wouldn't get ruined. But Mema put it back on today so you could see it when you came home. Do you really like it?"

"Yeah, you look cool."

"You should have seen this beautiful golden retriever at the grooming place. She left before I was done, so she didn't get to see how good I looked."

"Max, are you in love?"

"I could be. She said she has a guy, but I think she liked me a little."

"How could she not like you? You're such a handsome dog. And your big brown eyes, with that black around them that looks like eyeliner—you're gorgeous."

"Stop with the eyeliner stuff. I'm a guy. What's the scoop with Lynn? Did anything happen on the retreat?"

"Not really. Since Uncle Eric and Aunt Liza weren't back by the time we left on Friday, I pretended I didn't have my camera back yet, and I didn't take it with me, so there wouldn't be any problems with Lynn trying to take it. I don't think she would have done it anyway, Max. She seemed to have a really good time at the retreat."

"That's good."

"There is something odd, though. Lynn said she needed to talk to Khristian and me when we got back today, that it was really important. But Mom was already at the church waiting to pick us up, so we didn't get a chance to talk. Then she wanted me to come over to her house tonight, but of course Mom said I couldn't. I think she was crying, Max."

"Why?"

"I have no idea, and I probably won't see her until Wednesday, and that's if she decides to go to youth group with us."

"I don't like this at all," Max said. "We need to get this thing resolved. I wonder what's going on at the hellion children's house right now. What if she's in trouble for not getting the film? I don't want to think what might happen to her if those scruffy men get angry."

"Oh, Max! You don't think they'll hurt her, do you? And we have to stop calling it the hellion children's house."

"I hope not. But they sure looked mean, and they sounded even meaner." Max was interrupted by a loud clap of thunder. "What was that noise?" Max jumped up on AJ's bed and scrunched close to her.

"It was just thunder. Geez, Max. How can such a smart dog be so afraid of storms?"

"I am not afraid of storms. I just got up here because I wanted to be close to you. I missed you."

"Yeah, right. Then how come every time we get a little thunderstorm, you turn into a seventy-pound lap dog?"

"I told you, I am not afraid of storms," Max said indignantly. But at the next thunder-clap, he was nudging his head between AJ's arm and her side. He burrowed his nose into the palm of her hand."

"You big baby. Wait until I tell Khristian you're afraid of thunder."

"I am not afraid of thunder. It's just that the noise hurts my ears. Dogs have very sensitive hearing, you know."

By dinnertime, the thunderstorm was raging, and Max was as nervous as a student at FCAT (Florida Centralized Achievement Test) time. During dinner, Max squeezed under Papa's chair, not easy for a seventy-pound dog.

"Max, go lie down. There's not enough room for you here," Papa said. But it didn't do any good. Max stayed right where he was, and every time it thundered, he made these nervous little flopping moves. AJ thought she even heard him sigh. *Can dogs sigh?*

After dinner, Mema asked AJ to see if Max needed to go outside.

"Mema, you know he won't go out when it's storming."

"That's right," Amy said. "When it's storming, I think he can hold it for three days." Just then, there was a really huge blast of thunder, and Max jumped up and put his two front paws on Amy's lap and laid his head on his paws. "Poor baby." Amy put her arms around the trembling dog's neck. "You just don't understand what all that noise is, do you, Boy?"

See AJ, Max thought, *I'm not afraid. I just don't understand what the noise is.*

"Well," AJ said. "I've explained to him that there's nothing to be afraid of. But he just doesn't get it."

Mema, Papa and Amy started laughing. "Oh, you explained it, did you? What did he say when you were done explaining?" Mema asked.

"Oh, you know what I mean," AJ said. *I've got to remember that people don't hold conversations with dogs.*

Max and the Hurricane

"I sure hope that hurricane in the Caribbean doesn't come up into the Gulf. Max would probably have a heart attack if we had a hurricane," Papa said.

Max jerked his head toward Papa. *What's a hurricane? Is it like a thunderstorm?*

"They're predicting that it might. We'd better pull out our hurricane boxes and see if we need to replace anything," Mema said.

Amy pushed Max off her lap and went to the garage. She brought in several large storage boxes with hurricane supplies. "OK," she said, "here's a portable radio, batteries, paper plates, paper towels, a box of garbage bags, a wind-up clock, flashlights, some other portable lights, our old fashioned phone with a cord, and even the portable TV that Papa won in that contest."

"How much bottled water is left in the garage?" Papa asked Amy.

"Two five-gallon jugs, a couple of two-and-a-half-gallon jugs, and about five or six single-gallon jugs. Thank goodness we don't have to store water to flush the toilets. There's always water in the swimming pool and hot tub we can use for that," Amy said.

Mema said, "We need to get some more canned juices and soups. We said after Hurricane Charley hit Orlando that we were going to get a camp stove, and we never did. Let's get one tomorrow. I don't want to try cooking hot dogs over Sterno again."

Max looked from person to person as the conversation progressed. *What is going on? What are they talking about?*

"That didn't work too well. It took an hour just to get the water to boil, and we couldn't use the charcoal grill because it was raining too hard," Amy said.

"Let's not forget to prepare for our pets. Do we have extra food for Max and the cats?" Papa asked.

Max went over and laid his head in Papa's lap.

Thanks for thinking about me, Papa.

"I wish we had a generator," Mema said. "It seems like our power goes out at the drop of a hat, and I hate not having air conditioning."

"Tomorrow we'll get a small camp stove and let's start stocking up with ice and canned goods. If we're lucky we won't need them, but we don't want to be caught unprepared. Ivan is a monster storm. It's already a category four."

Max walked over and nipped AJ's hand and tried to pull her toward her bedroom. He wanted to talk to her about the storm. *What the heck was a category four, anyway? And who's Ivan?*

AJ finally got the hint and said, "You go ahead, Max. I'll be right there."

When AJ got to her room, Max was sitting in the middle of the floor with a worried look on his face. *I didn't know dogs could look worried,* AJ thought.

"Put a CD on to play so no one can hear us," Max said. "I have a lot of questions to ask you."

AJ sorted through her CDs, and Max started with his questions.

"What's a hurricane? What's a category four? Why did Papa say that we need to store some of my dog food? Will there be a lot of thunder? Who's Ivan? I don't want . . ."

"Whoa, big guy." AJ knelt down and put her arm around Max. "Hold on just a minute and I'll tell you everything. We just studied about hurricanes in science class. Hurricanes are big swirling storms. They have strong winds and lots of rain but hardly ever any thunder and lightning." AJ loaded the CD and turned up the volume.

"Oh, well. That's not so bad then, is it?"

"Well, they can be very bad. Hurricanes bring a ton of rain, and the winds are really strong. In a category four storm, like this one, the winds are between a hundred and thirty-one and a hundred and fifty-five miles an hour."

"If there's no thunder or lightning, what's the big deal?"

"A hundred and fifty-five mile-an-hour winds can rip things apart, even buildings. It could blow you over, and you're a big dog. Anything lying loose on the ground can be picked up by the strong winds and blown through the air like missiles, and that can hurt people if it hits them. The wind or the stuff blowing around can break windows. When that happens, people, or dogs, could be hurt by flying glass. The rains from hurricanes can cause flooding and something called a storm surge. That's when the wind causes a big wall of water, higher than most tides, sometimes even several stories high, to hit the shore."

"But there's no thunder?"

"No, Max. Most of the time, there's no thunder."

"Well, that doesn't sound so bad." Max sat up. "Why's everyone so upset about a big windstorm? And who's Ivan?"

"Well, strong winds have a tendency to break power lines, and that means no electricity. Broken live power lines hanging down are dangerous, too. People have been electrocuted from live power lines blowing in the wind."

"But you said no thunder, right?"

"No, Max. No thunder, most of the time."

"What do you mean 'most of the time'? You said no thunder!"

"You're such a baby. In science class we learned that the forward right quadrant . . . do you know what a quadrant is?"

"Du-uh! Get on with it."

"Well, the forward right quadrant, or the right front side in the direction the storm is traveling, that quadrant sometimes spawns tornados. Tornados can have thunder and lightning—tons of it."

"We're all gonna die!" Max yelled. He laid his head on the floor and put his two front paws on top of it.

"Quiet, Max! Do you want someone to hear you? We're not gonna die." AJ pulled Max's paws off of his head. "Sit up, you big wuss. Look, even if Ivan comes to the Tampa Bay area, we're not in an evacuation zone. We're in Zone E for evacuations."

"*Who's Ivan?* I don't care what zone we're in. I say we run for the hills—the hills of Georgia." Max paced back and forth across the room.

"Max, it'll be OK. I promise," AJ said.

"Sure, it'll be OK. That's why Mema is storing food. She wouldn't do that if it weren't going to be bad. You'd better tell Mema to get some extra Milk Bones. I don't want to have to go without my treats."

"Max! You're always thinking about your stomach, even when you're scared. I don't know which is worse, Max the worry wart worrying about the danger from the scruffy men, or Max the worry wart worrying about the possibility of a hurricane and no dog treats."

By Wednesday night, youth group at church was cancelled because Ivan was tracking straight for Tampa Bay. AJ and Khristian still had not been able to find out what Lynn wanted to talk to them about. They had each called her, but she said she wanted to talk to them, together, in person.

At the hellion children's house, the scruffy men were also making plans, but they weren't preparing for the hurricane.

Saheb's cousin called Sam and Saheb to a meeting. "Look, we still do not have that film from little Blondie. I think it's getting too hot to stay here, and I do not mean the weather.

"I know the main cell has plans to set off a number of explosions on the first day of the new year. I wanted our terror campaign to be bigger than any of theirs, so we could impress them. Maybe then, they would let us be part of the main cell. But now I am afraid that is too far away. We don't know who might have seen the picture that Blondie took of us. So we have to do something soon, something that will really impress them."

"What about the others? Will they sanction this change in plans?" Sam asked.

"We can't be the only group who is having problems keeping a—what do they call it? A low profile. Ever since nine-eleven, Americans are a lot more suspicious of strangers. What we need to do is select another big event where there will be a lot of people attending. We need to cause our ruckus and get out of the country quickly. The police could already be onto us. Do you have any ideas?"

When no one responded, Ali went on. "OK, Saheb, I want you to search the Internet for the state of Florida. See what you can find in the way of big events—lots of people, limited space. I don't want to wait any longer than, say, three weeks from today."

"Do not worry. I will be finding the proper event. Ali, are we going to tell Charles?"

"No. I do not trust him. All he cares about is staying out of jail."

Charles paced back and forth behind the lawnmower. *How can I stay out of jail? How can I protect my family? I know I done some bad things in the past, but I've never intentionally hurt nobody. If these guys get their way, hundreds, maybe even thousands of people might be hurt. And after it's over, they probably ain't gonna leave any witnesses. And we're all witnesses, not just me, but Annie and the kids, too. Maybe I should find some way to let the cops know what these guys are planning, then take my family and run so Ali can't find us.* Charles picked up a fallen branch and tossed it viciously over the fence. He wiped his face with his handkerchief and then resumed mowing.

They'd never let us get away. They keep too close a watch on us. Charles glanced toward the house and saw Sam watching him. It confirmed what he was thinking. *And they never let the whole family to leave the house at once. They always keep at least one family member here. They know we'd never run and leave anyone behind.*

"Sam," Saheb called, "look at this. I am thinking this would be perfect for what Ali is wanting. It is the annual football game between two Florida college enemies. See here? It says this is the biggest college game of the year in Florida."

"Which game is it?"

"It is the alligators eating the Indians," Saheb answered. "See this picture?"

"Alligators eating . . . ," Sam was confused until he looked at the picture. "Oh, the Gators-Seminoles game. That is a big event. When will it take place?"

"It says here it will be happening Saturday, November 20th. There are more than 83,000 people to be attending."

"I'll go tell Ali. It sounds like what he's looking for."

Charles put the mower away in the garage. He walked into the kitchen where Saheb was working on the computer and poured himself a glass of water. Saheb cleared the computer screen so Charles couldn't see what he was doing.

Charles leaned close to Saheb and whispered, "Saheb, what's goin on?"

"I am sorry, my friend. I cannot be telling you."

"Saheb, ain't you thought about this? If these guys git their way, a lotta people could be hurt, maybe even killed. It won't be just men, but women too, and even kids."

"No, I am trying not to be thinking about this. I am only thinking about saving my own bones."

"Skin, savin' yer skin, not bones. Well, you need ta think about it. We both do."

Lynn was hiding in the hallway and overheard the men talking. She ran to her room to think about what she could do.

I knew those men were up to no good. What am I going to do? How can I stop them? Oh God, if you're really up there, I need your help. How can I stop these men from hurting people and yet save my family? I don't know what to do. I'm so new at this praying stuff, but Amanda said prayer is just talking to God—so here I am, talking. I'm so scared. Help us, please help us!

The next day, AJ came in from school and complained to Max. "We're not having school tomorrow."

"Why not?"

"Because of this stupid hurricane. They're going to use all the public schools for shelters for people who are in evacuation areas."

"But you're not in public school. Are they going to use your school for a shelter, too?"

"No. But the school is in evacuation zone B. Allen's Creek that runs behind the school will flood if there's much of a storm surge. The creek is connected to Tampa Bay."

Max didn't want to believe what he was hearing. "But it's beautiful outside. This is the nicest day we've had for months. I can't believe there's a big storm coming."

"I know," AJ said, "but the storm is predicted to come ashore right over Tampa Bay tomorrow afternoon."

"I knew it," Max said. "We're all gonna die!"

"We're *not gonna die*," AJ yelled. Then she glanced out the kitchen window. "Hey! What's Mema doing home? And here comes Papa—and Mom, too. What's going on?" AJ and Max ran outside to greet everyone.

"Hi, Sweetie. Do you know if your school's closed tomorrow? I just heard on the car radio that all the public schools are closed," Mema asked when she got out of the van.

"Yeah, because of the storm. Is that why you guys are all home early?"

"Yes. My workplace is evacuation zone B, so they closed early, told us to come home to get ready for the storm. Since your mom works so close to me, I bet that's why she's home, too.

AJ ran over to the Jeep, and gave her mom a hug. Amy scratched Max's ears and asked AJ to take her things into the house, because she and Papa were going to get started closing all the hurricane shutters.

"While they're doing that, why don't we go out back and throw all the lawn furniture in the pool?" Mema said

Max was confused. Why were they going to throw the lawn furniture in the pool? Evidently, AJ was confused too.

"Mema, why are we throwing the lawn furniture in the pool?"

"That's what they said to do on TV. The lawn furniture is so light; it will blow around in the strong winds and could break windows or hurt someone. If we throw it in the pool, which won't hurt it because it's all plastic, it can't blow around."

"That's cool," AJ said.

AJ heaved a chair into the pool. "This is fun." She threw a table in after it. "But, maybe we should wait for a while. It's so nice today, maybe we could go swimming."

"We won't have time for that. We have too much to do. I stopped on the way home and picked up a few things, including batteries. I would like for you to get all the flashlights and radios out of the hurricane box and check them to see if they need new ones. I wish I could have gotten a camp stove, but they were sold out. We do have charcoal and some Sterno, but the charcoal is no good if it's raining, and the Sterno doesn't provide enough heat to cook with. Its main purpose is to keep things warm.

"Go get that little table at the other end of the patio, will you?"

When AJ went to get the table, Max followed so closely, he stepped on her heels. "What's with you, Max? I can't move without bumping into you."

"I want to know what's going on. I'm just trying to stay close. Do you think it's going to thunder and lightning soon?"

"Max, I thought I explained all that to you last night. Unless we're in the right front quadrant of the storm, we shouldn't have any thunder and lightning."

"Who are you talking to?" Mema asked.

"Max. I'm explaining that he doesn't need to be scared."

"He is acting kind of skittish. Come here, Max." Max walked over to Mema who gave him a hug. "You're such a big baby."

"Told ya," AJ said.

"AJ, you talk to Max as if he can talk back. You never had an imaginary friend when you were little. Is that what Max is?"

"No. But he's really smart. I know he understands us."

"Yeah, he's smart all right. Remember how we used to try to teach him to speak when he wanted out or in, or if he wanted a treat? He would never do it. Meeko was always the one to speak and then both of them got treats or went outside. Then, after Meeko died, Max started speaking to go out. I don't know if he's smart, letting Meeko do all the work, or just lazy."

Max's head jerked up, and he looked very offended when he looked at Mema. *Can dogs look offended?*

Hey, that hurts my feelings, Max thought. *Why should I have barked when Meeko did it for me? I'm smart, not lazy. Definitely smart.*

"It's OK, Max. Mema didn't mean to hurt your feelings," AJ patted the big dog's head.

Mema thought, *I swear, she treats that dog like he's human.*

After dinner that night, AJ got a call from Lynn.

"AJ, I need to talk to you and Khristian. It's really important."

"I don't know when we'll be together again with this storm and all. Can't you tell me what it's about?"

"I'd really rather talk to both of you."

"Well, I hope everything is back to normal by this weekend. Maybe we can get together then. Is your family ready for the hurricane?"

"I don't think they even know a hurricane is coming." *We have another kind of storm in this house.*

"Well, maybe you should say something to your mom and dad. We threw all our lawn furniture in the pool. That's to keep it from blowing around. And we put our hurricane shutters down, and we made sure all of our radios and flashlights have fresh batteries . . ."

Lynn knew if she didn't interrupt, AJ would go on forever. "I have to go now, AJ. I'll try to talk to you tomorrow."

"OK. Be safe," AJ disconnected the call and phoned Khristian. When he answered the phone, she asked him about their hurricane preparations first.

"Are you guys all ready for the big storm?"

"My mom and dad just called me. They're at Home Depot waiting in line to get some plywood for the windows. They've been there since five o'clock."

"Wow. I'm glad we have hurricane shutters. All we have to do is close them when a storm comes. Did they say how much longer they'd be?"

"My dad said there were only three more people in front of them, but they have to wait for another truck to come in."

"Bummer. Do you want to come over here for a while? Then you won't have to wait for them alone."

"I don't think I can. My mom gave me a big paper to write before they left. She said with the storm, we probably wouldn't have school tomorrow, so she wants me to get it done tonight, at least a rough draft."

"Man, she's worse than the teachers at school. When they told us we wouldn't have school tomorrow, they also said that any assignments given today wouldn't be due until two days after we're back in school. Tell your mom to lighten up."

"Yeah, right. Then I'll be grounded forever. I think I'll just work on my paper."

"I wish you could come over. Since the bad weather hasn't started yet, maybe we could go over to Lynn's house. She just called and she sounds really upset. She said she wants to talk to us."

"Won't she tell you what's wrong?"

"No. She said she wants to talk to both of us. That's why I called you. Maybe if this storm blows through and things are back to normal by the weekend, you can come over and we can talk to her then."

"Sounds like a plan. I'd better get back to my paper. If my mom comes home and I'm not done, I'll be in trouble. Hey, that gives me an idea."

"What's that?"

"Remember when we were talking about that face recognition program the police have?"

"Yeah, what about it?"

"What if we told your Uncle Eric that I have to write a paper, and I want to write it on the face recognition software? I could ask him for help with my research. Hopefully, he'll take us to the Sheriff's Department and we can figure out a way to use the face recognition software to try to find out who those guys at Lynn's house are?"

"I don't know if he has anything to do with that software, but it's worth a try."

"Let's talk about it some more this weekend. Right now I need to get my rough draft on this paper done before my mom gets home."

After they hung up, AJ called Max to follow her and went into her bedroom and shut the door.

"What's up?" Max asked.

"Lynn called and she's really upset. She wants to talk to Khristian and me. She won't tell me what's wrong because she wants to talk to us together. Max, do you suppose they did something to her because she didn't get the film?"

"I don't know. It doesn't sound good. Did she say anything else?"

"No, just that she wanted to talk to Khristian and me together. I have an idea, though."

"This better be good."

"What if we gave Lynn the camera? I could call her back and tell her that Uncle Eric just brought it back to me. We can put the disk back in the camera with the pictures from the Halloween party. I'll tell her that she can take the disk and look at the pictures on her computer. Then, if the scruffy men want to, they can delete the picture they don't want us to have, and all this will be over."

"I see two problems with your idea. One, they don't know you have a digital camera. They think you have film that hasn't been developed yet. If they think that we've seen the pictures, you and K could be in more danger."

"OK, let's think about that one in a minute. What's the second problem?"

"Two, as much as I hate to say it, we need to stay involved. We don't have any idea what those men have planned, and we don't know why they don't want us to see the picture. Are they common criminals or something worse?"

"What's worse?"

"Well, when you three were in the pool that first day and I was under the kitchen window listening, I heard them talking."

"I know that. You made a big deal about telling us. You about scared Khristian to death."

"What I didn't tell you is that I heard them call one of the men by name."

"What's the big deal?"

"Well, Sam's real name is Sharif. That's a very Arabic sounding name. I don't want to label anyone as a terrorist just because they have an Arabic name, but we already know the men are some kind of criminals. What if they're part of a terrorist group?"

"I never thought about that. That's really scary, Max."

"Now maybe you understand better why I've been so upset."

"We need to talk to Lynn. I hope this storm blows over soon."

"Me, too," Max said. "Me, too. Now, are you sure there won't be any thunder?"

"MAX!"

"You know, Khristian has an idea. Remember when we were working on the computer with the photo program?"

"Of course."

"Khristian wants to tell Uncle Bubbie that he has to write a paper and he wants to write it on the face recognition software the sheriff's department uses. You know what a computer geek Khristian is. Then, he would ask Uncle Eric to help him with his research. Maybe even get him to take K to the Sheriff's Department and show him how their computers work with the software."

"That's probably the best idea so far. Let's wait to see what happens after this storm is over. Maybe we can make use of that."

The next morning the weather was overcast and it rained off and on. The wind was already gusting to about thirty miles an hour. Amy and Papa were outside taping the glass patio doors, and Mema was working inside the house getting ready for the storm.

Max couldn't decide what to do. He went outside and followed Papa and Amy, and then he wanted back inside where he followed Mema around the house. Then he wanted to go back outside again.

"Max, you've got to settle down and make up your mind. Do you want to be inside or outside?" Mema was losing patience with Max because she was too busy to keep letting him in and out. "AJ, why don't you take Max out back and see if we've left anything on the ground that the wind could pick up."

AJ and Max went outside and walked around the pool to the far end of the yard.

"Max, why are you so jumpy?" AJ asked.

"Me, jumpy? I'm not jumpy. But Mema, Papa, and your mom sure are nervous about this storm. Dogs pick up on these things, you know?"

"Yeah, I guess they are a little nervous. I'm feeling kind of scared myself. Do you dogs get that funny feeling in the pit of your stomach when you're kind of scared?"

"We sure do. Especially when our humans are worried or scared. I'm only going to ask you this one more time, are you sure there won't be any thunder and lightning in this hurricane?" Just then, a much stronger gust of wind howled, and a lid from someone's garbage can flew over the fence, just missing AJ and Max. AJ screamed and Max yelped. Both ran back into the house and told Mema what happened.

"It's probably a good idea if we all stay in the house from now on. The wind is getting much stronger, and that garbage can lid won't be the only thing flying around. Papa is going to fix us a big breakfast so we'll have a good meal in case the power goes out and we can't cook later."

After the family ate breakfast and cleaned up, there really wasn't much to do, except to wait for the storm. Around one-thirty, they heard the first sound, like a gunshot, signaling the first power transformer to blow out in the storm.

"What was that?"

"Relax, Max. It was one of the power transformers. You know they always blow out in a storm."

"Are you sure it wasn't thunder?"

"Max, get off that subject. It wasn't thunder. Why are you so scared of thunder?"

"I told you, it hurts my ears. I'm not scared."

Just then, a second transformer blew, and then a third. Max squeezed next to AJ and laid his head on her lap. Shortly, everyone heard a fourth transformer blow, and that's when the power went out. Since the windows were covered with storm shutters, the house was very dark. AJ and Max jumped up and ran out to the screened-in porch where Papa and Mema were reading.

"Whoa, you two are moving pretty fast. Did you get scared?" Mema asked.

"No, we're not afraid," AJ said. "We just came out to see if you needed any help. It sure got dark in the house fast."

"That's because it's so cloudy and all the windows are covered. We should probably light the lantern and some candles throughout the house. Do you have your flashlight, or did you run out here so fast you forgot it?"

AJ looked kind of sheepish. "I forgot you put one in my bedroom. I just ran out when the power went off."

"Why don't you go get it, and keep it with you?"

"Would you come with me? You can light the oil lamp in the bathroom." AJ was kind of scared of the dark and didn't want anyone to know it, but Mema understood.

"Come on, let's go get it."

Mema started back into the house with AJ and Max close on her heels. They met Amy coming up the hallway."

"I've got the oil lamps in my bedroom and the bathroom lit. AJ, here's your flashlight. I found it in your room."

"Are you going to put an oil lamp in my room?" AJ asked.

"I don't think that's a good idea. We have to be very careful of fire. It would be a shame if our house survived the storm undamaged but burned down because we were careless with candles and oil lamps."

"Why don't you get one of your books and join us on the porch. We can sit out there and read. It's going to get pretty hot in here with no AC and the windows closed and boarded up."

AJ, Papa, and Mema spent the afternoon on the porch reading. Amy took a nap because she and Papa were awake so early to finish the windows. Max roamed back and forth between Amy's room and the porch.

"Poor Max. He can't seem to be still. I think he's afraid of the storm," Papa said.

"He's not the only one. Papa, are we safe?"

"Well, Honey, we're as safe as we can be. We've followed all the preparations in the hurricane guide, and this is a pretty sturdy house. I think we'll be just fine. Hey! Here's Orco and Brownie. That's weird. Those two cats don't usually come out in the middle of the day."

"It's so dark in the house, they probably think it's nighttime," AJ said.

Oreo walked over to Max and tried to lie down right next to him. When he did, Max got up and moved. Oreo got up and moved next to him again.

"Max and Oreo are doing their dance again," Mema said.

"I don't know why he won't let Oreo lay next to him. Oreo loves Max."

Brownie just sat under a small table peeking out at everyone. She looked confused. *Can cats look confused?* AJ thought.

Max kept moving, and Oreo kept trying to lie down next to him. Max didn't seem to like Oreo much.

AJ took her flashlight and went down the hall and peeked into her mom's room. She saw that her mom was asleep. Max, again, was right on AJ's heels.

"Max, why won't you let Oreo lay next to you? He's probably scared, too."

"I told you, I'm not scared. I just don't like that cat. He's sneaky."

"He is not. He's a sweetheart . . . and he's very lovable, for a cat. Brownie is the sneaky one. She even looks sneaky. Wait a minute, that's not fair. Brownie's a tortoiseshell cat. She can't help it if her coloring and her face remind me of an owl, a mean owl. Why do you like her and not Oreo? Just look at him, he's such a cutie. I love the way his face is half black and half white. It looks like someone drew a line down his face from his left eyebrow to his right cheek. He's so adorable."

"Adorable? I don't think so. Every time that cat gets near me, he tries to groom me," Max complained. "And you must be nervous too, you're talking a lot, and very fast."

"That's what cats do, groom. And I am not talking a lot."

"Well, no self-respecting dog will allow it, but he just doesn't seem to get the hint."

"Max, you're getting cranky in your old age. Why don't you go lie down? Don't you usually sleep all day?"

"I'm sticking close to you, to make sure you're safe."

"Yeah, right. Let's go back out and see what Mema and Papa are doing."

When they got to the porch, Papa said, "Let's turn on the little battery operated TV and get a weather update."

What they heard was good news, kind of. The storm had turned a bit and was only going to skim the coast, not come directly on shore. The bad news was that the power company announced that they would not send crews out to restore power until the hurricane had completely cleared the area. As slow as the storm was moving, that could be another day or so.

"I hate that sound the wind makes whipping through the electrical wires," AJ said. "It sounds like a ghost moaning."

"How do you know what a ghost moaning sounds like?" Mema teased.

"You know what I mean. It gives me the creeps." Just then a gust of wind stronger than any so far blew through the area.

"Wow! Look at the branches in that big live oak tree. I didn't think those big branches could bend so far."

A loud cracking noise from in front of the house interrupted her. AJ, Papa, Mema, and Max ran to look out the front door.

"I guess some of those branches don't bend that far," Papa said. Behind one of the houses across the street, a huge live oak tree had split down the middle, the halves falling on each side of the house but doing no damage to the house itself.

"That's a miracle," Mema said. "I don't see any damage."

Papa said, "Nobody's home over there. They went to stay with their parents in Orlando. Wait till they see how lucky they are that big tree missed their house."

"This is getting really freaky." AJ wrapped her arm around Max who was plastered against her leg.

"We should probably eat something. It'll be dark soon," Mema said.

Mema made peanut butter and jelly sandwiches, Amy sliced apples for dessert, and Papa poured everyone some sweet tea.

AJ got out the paper plates and napkins. "This is fun," she said. "Kind of like camping out."

"I never liked camping," Mema said.

Papa added. "Mema's idea of roughing it is a Holiday Inn with no room service."

"Now what are we going to do? I'm bored. What did people do in the old days with no electricity, Mema?"

"Young lady, I'll have you know I'm not that old. We had electricity when I was your age. We even got a TV when I was in first grade."

"First grade! What did you do without TV?"

"We listened to the radio, played board games or cards, and we read a lot. We also talked to one another."

"I've been reading all day. I want to do something else. I'm so bored. I can't watch TV. I can't play games on the computer. I can't talk to my friends in the chat room. The cordless phone doesn't work . . ."

"Stop whining. At least we still have a roof over our heads," Amy said. And under her breath she added "for now anyway." She added that because the wind had picked up quite a bit and was screaming through the trees.

Everyone decided to go to bed early. Although they didn't want to admit it to AJ, the adults were bored too. The house was stifling with no AC, and with the windows boarded up, it was very dark. The only breeze came from the open glass doors to the screened in porch and the open front door. There was an alley of air straight through the center of the living room from the front door to the screened-in porch.

"AJ, let's get the mattress off the futon in the TV room and sleep in the living room," her mom said.

"Great! I really don't want to sleep in my room by myself either."

The two of them dragged the mattress off of the futon into the living room where they put it in the middle of the floor. Mema tried to sleep on the living room couch, but it was just too hot lying on the leather couch. Papa dozed off and on in his recliner, but every hour or so he would get up, grab a flashlight, and make the rounds of the house and yard, checking for damage. Max stuck so close that Papa kept stepping on his paws as he was making his rounds. It was a miserable night.

The next morning Uncle Eric called. "No, we didn't lose power. I'm surprised, with all the huge trees around our house. I thought for sure one of the big branches would get blown off the tree and pull down some power lines, but none did. Why don't you all come over here?"

"You don't have to ask me twice," Amy said. She gave the phone to Mema and told AJ to pack a few things.

Mema hung up the phone and went to find Amy. "Dad and I aren't going to go with you over to Eric and Liza's."

"Why not? I know you hate the heat, and it's supposed to be really hot today".

"We need to stay here and wait for the power company. We have to make sure the AC and all the appliances are working when the power comes back on."

Amy and AJ loaded their overnight bags and Max into the Jeep and went to Eric and Liza's.

"Do we have any damage outside?" Mema asked Papa.

"Just a few pieces of fence that were blown over. I think the posts are broken and will have to be replaced."

"It's so dark in here," Mema said. "I never realized how dark the hurricane shutters would make it. And it's so hot. I'd kill for a battery operated fan."

The storm hit Tampa Bay on Friday, and the Harveys didn't get their power turned back on until the next Tuesday. On Sunday, Mema and Papa gave up and went to stay with the rest of the family at Eric and Liza's.

When they arrived, AJ wanted to know why they didn't bring Oreo and Brownie.

"Honey, cats are such independent creatures, they'll be fine at home. We left them plenty of food and water, and you and mom can stop by every day to give them more. Don't you think we're imposing enough on your aunt and uncle? Now we have five adults, you, three dogs and Eric and Liza's two cats. This is only a small two-bedroom house."

They were very crowded. Mema and Papa slept on a futon in the den, and Amy and AJ slept on blow-up air mattresses on the living room floor. Everything was so confusing AJ forgot about the mystery. Even Max seemed too preoccupied to worry about the scruffy men.

Monday afternoon, AJ took Max outside to talk to him. "Are you OK, Max?" AJ asked. "You don't seem like yourself."

"No, I'm not OK. Misha is making my life miserable. All she does is growl and snap at me, especially when I try to get near the food dish."

"Growl back. You have to put her in her place. Don't you remember when Uncle Eric first got her? She treated Mick the same way. He had to get really mean with her a few times before she backed down and accepted him."

"It's just not in my nature to be mean, and I don't like confrontations."

"I think you're just too lazy to put her in her place. I don't know why she acts like that with you. She's really a sweetie. Very lovable."

"With humans. But she doesn't like any other dogs but Mick. Don't worry; I can tolerate her until we get home."

Mick happened to be coming around the corner of the house, and he heard Max talking to AJ. *Wow, Max is one of the special ones. I've heard of other animals that could talk, but talking to a human? It is forbidden. I can't believe my ears. Max has broken the Animal Code of Silence.*

Later, when all three dogs were outside and no humans were around, Mick confronted Max about speaking to humans.

"I didn't have any choice," Max said.

"I always knew he was riff-raff," Misha sniffed.

"Be quiet! We don't need any of your sass right now," Mick told her. Then he turned back to Max.

"Max, this is serious. If it gets out, you'll be shunned by all the other animals. Do Oreo and Brownie know you can talk to humans?"

"Oreo does, and he hasn't shunned me. I wish he would. I don't think Brownie knows, but she and I are pretty tight. Look, Mick, I didn't have any choice. AJ and Khristian are in danger. There are some very bad men who want to hurt them."

"Let's go get them," Misha said. "Nobody's going to hurt our humans."

"Down, girl," Mick said. "Let's hear the whole story. Max?"

After Max told Mick and Misha everything that had happened, they still weren't convinced Max had done the right thing.

"Did you have to talk to both of them? Couldn't you have just told AJ?"

"Nah. They're together all the time, which puts them both in danger. Do you think I wanted to get into this mess? I was perfectly content just living my life as a normal dog. I don't need this aggravation. But I couldn't let the kids be hurt if I could help them. Are you two going to shun me?"

"I'm not," Mick said. "Let me know if there's anything I can do to help".

"I never liked you anyway," Misha said, "so I don't see any reason to treat you any differently than I ever have. I do love those kids though. You'd better not let anything happen to them," she growled.

"That's what worries me. What if I can't stop them from getting hurt?"

Mick and Misha didn't have any answers for Max.

Tuesday the family moved back home and things started getting back to normal. The big game was only two weeks away, and Liza was able to get enough tickets so that AJ could invite both Khristian and Lynn to the game.

To Tell—or Not to Tell

After Khristian's parents gave him permission to attend the game, AJ called Lynn to invite her. But Lynn said she was busy and couldn't talk just then.

At the hellion children's house, Lynn paced back and forth in her bedroom. She was in a quandary about what to do. *There's no way I can stand by and let people be hurt by whatever these scruffy men are planning. What if their target is the Gators-Seminole game?* Lynn went looking for her dad.

"Where is everyone?" she asked him.

"Mom's taken the boys to a birthday party at one of their friend's house. Saheb and Ali went somewhere in the van. That leaves only Sharif, I mean Sam. I keep forgettin' that's what we're supposed to call him."

"Well, he's snoring on the couch. Dad, I have to talk to you—in private."

"Let's go outside so's Sam won't hear us. I need ta clean the pool."

Lynn sat on a lawn chair while her dad hooked up the pool vacuum.

"Dad, I know those men are planning to do something soon, and you can't let them."

"Lynn, ya need ta mind yer own business. That don't concern ya."

"But, Dad, it does concern me. First, those guys wanted to hurt my friends. Now, they're going to hurt a bunch of people at some kind of big public gathering. How can you be part of this? I just don't understand."

Charles didn't say anything as he wound the hose up and hung it on a hook.

"Honey, ya know I love ya."

"I know, but what about all those people? I heard those men say eighty-thousand people. Dad, you can't let this happen. You just can't. If you let this happen, I'll never forgive you."

"Lynn, I bin tryin' ta figure out what ta do. Don't cha realize these guys'll hurt you kids or yer mom if I don't do what they say?"

"Dad, AJ invited me to go to the Gators-Seminole game with her family. What if the target was something like that?"

"Can't you talk em outta goin'? I don't know what the target is, but jus' now I wouldn't wanna go to any big doin's."

"Are you kidding? You'd think they won the lottery; they're so excited about that stupid game. There's no way they'll miss it. Daddy, what if I go? Will you still let those men hurt people—maybe at that game?"

"Honey, no. Ya know I wouldn't. I just don't know what ta do. Lemme think on it for a while, try ta come up with a plan so's nobody gets hurt—not you kids or yer mom and not yer friends."

"OK, Dad. But that game is in two weeks. And whatever these guys are planning is in two weeks. Please, think of something fast."

"Max, that was really weird," AJ said as she hung up the phone. "It was like Lynn couldn't wait to get off the phone with me. I thought she'd be excited that we had enough tickets so that she could go to the Gators-Seminole game with us, but she said she didn't think she'd be able to go."

"Well, maybe her family has something planned," Max answered.

"She didn't even leave the phone to go and ask. When Khristian gets here, we need to go over there. She's wanted to talk to the two of us since the retreat. Maybe we can find out why she's so upset."

"You're not thinking of going over there without me, are you?"

"No. I know you'd be worried. When Khristian gets here, we'll say we're taking you for a walk and stop by to see if she wants to join us and take her dog, Buddy, for a walk."

"Not that rambunctious pup! He's so obnoxious. I swear, he acts just as wild as those hellion brothers of hers."

"Max, I asked you to stop calling them that. Besides, Buddy's not so bad. He just has a lot of energy."

"A lot of energy? Mick has a lot of energy. Buddy's a pain in the neck. He runs around like an idiot, gets his leash all tangled up, barks at everything . . . ," Max was interrupted by a sneeze.

"God bless you. Boy, you really are getting cranky in your old age. Are you getting a cold?"

Max didn't answer; he just walked away, mumbling to himself.

I didn't know dogs could mumble, AJ thought.

AJ's plans to visit Lynn didn't work out, because Khristian didn't arrive until it was almost time to leave for the movies.

"Why are you so late?" AJ complained. "I thought you were going to get here an hour ago."

"I didn't have my history outline finished, and my mom said I couldn't come over until it was done."

"Man, she's really a tough teacher. The bad thing is, now we don't have time to go over to Lynn's house."

"I know. Sorry. Why don't you ask her if she wants to go to the movies with us? That's if it's OK with your mom."

"I already did. She said she had something to do tonight. I get the feeling she's avoiding me."

"At least I don't have to put up with that nuisance, Buddy," Max said. Then he sneezed twice. The second time, he sneezed so hard he bumped his head on the floor.

"Ouch, that had to hurt," Khristian said. "Are you getting sick?"

"I don't know. I can't seem to stop sneezing."

"Come here," AJ said. "Let me feel your nose."

Max walked over and put his head in her hand. "Your nose does feel kind of warm and it's dry. I'd better tell Mema that you might be getting sick."

"I'm fine. Don't want to go to the vet's."

"Are you scared of the vet like you're scared of thun—der?" Khristian teased.

"AJ! You said you wouldn't tell." Max growled. To Khristian he said, "I am NOT afraid of thunder. It just hurts my ears." Max sneezed again.

"That's it. I'm telling Mema you're sick." AJ went to find her grandmother.

By the time AJ and Khristian got home from the movies, Max wasn't feeling well at all. They found him sleeping in Amy's shower, his favorite spot to nap. He liked it because when he was in the shower, there wasn't any room for Oreo to try to sleep next to him. AJ and Khristian were trying to wake him up when Amy came into her bedroom.

"Why don't you guys let him sleep? We gave him some of that allergy medicine the vet gave us, and it makes him sleepy."

The next day after church, Khristian and AJ resurrected their plan to take a walk with Lynn and her dog, Buddy.

AJ knocked on the door of Lynn's house, and Lynn's mom came to the door.

"Hi, Mrs. Cranston. We wondered if Lynn and Buddy want to go for a walk with us."

"That's nice of you. Let me go get her."

But when she went back into the house and told Lynn the kids were there, Lynn told her mom to tell them she was still sleeping.

"I will not lie to them, young lady. Besides, the exercise would be good for Buddy. Maybe it will tire him out and he won't be so wild."

So Lynn wrestled with Buddy and put on his collar and leash. She tugged him out the door and joined AJ and Khristian. While Max walked sedately next to Khristian, Buddy was jerking on his leash, practically forcing Lynn to run.

"Hey! Wait up," AJ called, running to catch up with them. But Buddy saw a squirrel and tore off after it, dragging Lynn along with him.

By the time they reached the small park with the pond, all three kids were exhausted from trying to keep Buddy under control. Lynn tied him to the leg of the picnic table and plopped down on the bench.

"He needs to go to obedience training," AJ said dropping down next to her.

"Definitely—that or tranquilizers," Khristian added. He sat on the ground facing the girls, and Max lay down next to him.

"Max is so well-behaved," Lynn said. "Did he go to obedience school?"

"No. And he used to be just as wild as Buddy," AJ said. Max jerked his head up and gave her a dirty look.

Is he giving me a dirty look, AJ thought?

Khristian said, "He was worse. He used to slip out of his collar, no matter how tight we put it. Then we'd have to chase him down. He was really fast, too." Max lifted his head and sneezed and Khristian said, "Yuck! He slimed me," and wiped his arm on his pants.

"Sorry," Max whispered to Khristian.

"You knew AJ when Max was a puppy? How long have you guys been friends?" Lynn asked.

"Since we were five. Meeko and Max were only two years old then, and they were both pretty wild. They ate my grandma's couch. Whenever we'd try to take them for a walk, we spent all our time chasing Max."

"Maybe there's hope for Buddy yet," Lynn said. "Max is so quiet now; you'd never know he used to be wild. I thought he was either very well-behaved or just lazy."

Now he's giving Lynn a dirty look. I need to talk to him about this.

"Lynn, you've been asking to talk to Khristian and me together. Well, here we are. Let's talk."

Lynn burst into tears, and AJ and Khristian exchanged astonished looks. Khristian, typical boy, looked away embarrassed. He didn't deal well with tears. AJ tried to put her arm around Lynn, but the other girl pulled away from her, so she just patted her knee until Lynn seemed to regain control.

"What's wrong?" AJ asked, and Lynn began sobbing again.

"Do something," Khristian mouthed to AJ.

"What?" she mouthed back. Khristian just shrugged his shoulders. Max got up and walked over to Lynn and laid his head in her lap.

They all just sat there for a few minutes until Lynn seemed to settle down again. She put her arm around Max's neck and gave him a hug. Then she sat up straight and said, "I have something I need to tell you, but if I do, I could cause my family to get hurt. But if I don't, you could be hurt. I don't want to put my family in danger, but you've both been so nice to me, I don't want you to get hurt either. I'm so confused."

"Does this have anything to do with those scruffy guys who're staying at your house?" Khristian asked.

Lynn covered her face and began sobbing again.

"Now see what you've done," AJ snapped at Khristian.

"I didn't do anything. All I did was ask a question. Girls!"

Lynn jumped up and untied Buddy's leash from the picnic table leg. "I'm sorry. I'm so sorry," she said. Then she turned and ran all the way home, for once with Buddy struggling to keep up.

Khristian said, "I think there's more going on than just those guys trying to get your camera, AJ."

"Yeah, me too. But what can we do about it?"

"Well, that settles it," Max said. "Did you hear that part about either her family would get hurt or you two would get hurt? As much as I hate the idea, we're going to have to get the adults involved. I really hoped it wouldn't come to this."

"Max, we can't. What will we tell them?"

"The truth. I'm beginning to think we should have done it a long time ago."

"What truth?" Khristian asked. "That you overheard those scruffy guys talking so you warned AJ and me? That'll go over great. I thought you didn't want the adults to know you can talk."

"We don't have any choice. You heard Lynn. You two could be hurt and it sounds like her family is in danger, too. Are Uncle Bubbie and Aunt Liza coming for dinner tonight?"

"Yes. Mema said it's a thank-you dinner for letting all of us stay at their house last week when we didn't have any power. Papa's cooking steaks on the grill."

"Well, why don't you two tell them that after dinner you have a little play you want to put on for them. Like you used to do when you were little. We'll get them all in the living room, and then we'll break the news to them." Max sneezed.

"God bless you. Hey! You were the one worried about talking in front of the adults. If you want to break your Animal Code of Silence again, that's your decision."

AJ, Khristian, and Max returned home and found that Uncle Eric and Aunt Liza were already there. Mick and Misha were with them, along with Aunt Liza's sister, Tatianna and her two-year-old, Julianne. With six adults, three kids, three dogs, and two cats milling around, things were pretty crazy. The kids didn't have a chance to talk to Max again before dinner.

"Where's Max?" Mema asked as they all sat down to eat.

"He's sleeping in my shower," Amy said. "He was still sneezing, so I gave him some more of that medicine for his allergies."

"Khristian and I have a short play for everyone after dinner. We need Max for it, though. Do you think he'll be awake by then?"

"Is he the star of the show?" Papa asked.

"You might say that," Khristian said. AJ kicked him under the table. "Ouch! That hurt."

"You two fight like brother and sister," Aunt Liza said.

"I remember when they were about five," Mema added. "Khristian came over to spend the day with AJ after bowling, and they wanted to go to the park. Amy had a migraine, so I took them to Largo Central Park. They still had on their purple tee shirts from bowling and some lady said, 'Oh, your twins are so cute'."

"Twins! We don't look like twins," Khristian snorted. "I'm a boy, and I'm a lot bigger than AJ."

"Not now, you don't. You've gotten so much taller than AJ, and your hair has gotten a lot darker. But back then you were both the same size, and your hair was much lighter, almost blond. You both had on purple tee-shirts and black shorts. I don't know about twins, but you sure could have passed for brother and sister."

After dinner, AJ and Khristian worked hard to get the family gathered in the living room for the big reveal. But it seemed that every time they got two or three people in there, someone was missing. They finally had everyone but Uncle Eric. He'd just taken Mick and Misha outside.

"Uncle Eric, we need you in here," AJ yelled out the door. She was nervous and getting very frustrated.

"Khristian, go wake Max up," she said. "Mema, where are you going? We need you to stay here."

"I'm just getting a cup of coffee. I'll be back before Eric gets in with the dogs."

"Aunt Liza, where are you going?"

"My cell phone is ringing. I'll just get it from my purse and be right back."

AJ crossed her arms and rolled her eyes. Khristian came back into the living room with a very sleepy looking Max. "I don't think Max feels too well," he whispered.

Baby Julianne said, "Hi, Max." She was just beginning to talk, and Max came out as three separate syllables. It was so cute.

AJ knelt down and put her arm around Max. "Are you OK? You sure you want to do this?" Max didn't answer.

"OK," Papa said. "We're all here. You can start your play."

AJ turned around to see the six adults looking at the two kids and Max expectantly.

She stood up slowly, and began, "Well, it's not really a play. It's more like we need to talk to all of you about something." Max nipped her hand and tried to pull her back toward the hallway. "Stop it, Max. You'll get your turn." Mick walked over and tried to get Max to play with him. "Stop it, Mick. *Eric, can't you control him?*" AJ was so nervous that she was screaming.

"Cool it, AJ," Eric said. "The dogs are just being dogs. Settle down." Suddenly, it got very quiet and still in the room.

"Sorry. We're a little nervous," Khristian said.

"You've put on hundreds of little plays for us. What are you so nervous about?" Papa asked.

"This isn't really a little play," Khristian said. "This is . . . well, I'm not really sure what this is."

"Look, you guys remember my Halloween party?" AJ interrupted.

"Sure, you and twenty-four of your closest friends," Aunt Liza said. "It was crazy."

"Well, something happened that night. Uncle Eric, remember on the scavenger hunt when we went to the hellion children's house and Max was growling and barking?"

"How could I forget? It wasn't like Max at all. He was acting more like Misha."

"Tell me about it. Well, I had my new camera that night, and I was taking pictures. I took a picture at their house just when Lynn's dad opened the door and yelled at us to get off his property. Remember that?"

"Kind of. So?"

"You and Aunt Liza left on vacation the next day, so you don't know what happened after that."

"What happened?"

"Khristian and I were taking Max for a walk, and when we went by the hellion children's house, Lynn, she's the oldest kid, asked us if we wanted to come over for a swim. They have a heated pool."

"I thought you didn't like those kids."

"Well, I didn't used to, but that day, Lynn was nice. So we invited her over here for supper that night. Then the next day, Khristian, Max, and I went over there for another swim."

"Max went for a swim? Max actually got off his duff and went for a swim?" Uncle Eric joked. Max looked offended. *Can dogs look offended?*

"No, he didn't swim. He took a nap on their patio while we swam."

"That sounds more like Max. Is there a point to this story?"

"Yes, but it's not easy. Just give me a minute. Khristian, maybe you should tell them."

"I'm not telling them, you tell them. You're the one who likes to talk so much."

"Maybe Max should tell them."

"Yeah," Eric said sarcastically. "You tell us, Max."

Everyone looked at Max who just lay down and put his head on his front paws. The silence seemed to go on forever.

"Come on, Max. This was your idea," Khristian said.

"Yeah. Come on, Max. Tell them what you told us," AJ added.

Silence.

"Max!"

"All right. This isn't funny. If you two don't have a play for us, I'm going to do the dishes," Mema said.

"Max," AJ yelled, "tell them!"

More silence.

"That's enough," AJ's mom said. "Can't you see he's sick? You can put your play on some other time. If he's not better by tomorrow, I'm taking him to the vet. Come on, Max. You can go back to sleep now." She took Max's collar and led him back to her bedroom.

AJ and Khristian just stared at each other. They didn't know what to say. They heard a car in the driveway and looked out to see that Khristian's mom was there to pick him up. The kids went into AJ's room to get his things together.

"I don't get it," AJ said. "It was his idea. Why wouldn't he say anything? Here, don't forget your pillow."

"Maybe he just changed his mind. It is a really big deal to him, you know." Khristian rolled his pillow up in his sleeping bag.

"I know, but it was his idea. What are we going to do now?"

"I've got to go home. Call me after you get a chance to talk to him."

That night, Max wouldn't even come out of Amy's shower to go outside. Amy was in her room watching TV, so AJ couldn't talk to Max. She was very confused and felt like crying.

Khristian called later.

"If he wasn't sick, I'd wring his neck," AJ said.

"I'm getting scared," Khristian said. "Remember what Lynn said about her family being in danger, or us being in danger. I wish we could talk to her and try to find out what's going on."

"Me, too. I tried to call her after you left, but she said she couldn't talk. If we try to tell the adults what's going on now, after tonight's fiasco, I wonder if they'll believe us."

"Is your Uncle Eric still there?"

"Yeah, but they're getting ready to leave. Why?"

"I think we need to try my other idea."

"What other idea?"

"You know, the one where I ask your uncle Eric to help me write a paper on the face recognition software. At least that might help us find out who those guys are. Then, maybe we'd know what to do."

"I forgot about that. I think that's a great idea. Hang on, and I'll go tell him you need his help."

AJ came back to the phone in a few minutes. "K?"

"I'm here. What took so long?"

"I had to wait until he was done talking to my grandpa. He said he'd be glad to help you. He needs more information, though."

"Let me put something together. Since I really do have to write a research paper, maybe I can tie it into that for real. Then I won't have to research something else.

"In the morning, I'll ask my mom to give me the instructions for that new research paper—tell her I want to get started early. That ought to get me some brownie points. I'll call you when you get home from school tomorrow, and we'll figure out how to get your uncle to let us use the software. Maybe we can run that picture through it and find out who those guys are."

"Mr. K, you're a genius. Talk to you tomorrow."

At the hellion children's house, things were extremely tense. Now that the scruffy men had a specific plan, they were nervous and cranky. They spent a lot of time in the garage working on something in the back of Charles's old van. Charles suspected they might be putting together some kind of explosive device.

Ali no longer spoke to Charles, except to snarl at him when he needed to find another tool. Saheb was working in the van, and Sam was standing guard at the garage door.

"Dad, will you go with me to take Buddy for a walk? He's so wild; I can't handle him by myself."

Charles started to refuse Lynn's request, but she was pleading with him with her eyes. So he decided to go. He told Sam that his wife and the boys were inside and that he and Lynn were taking the dog for a walk.

Once they were out of earshot of the house, Lynn began.

"Dad, have you thought of any way to get us out of this mess yet? Buddy, stop!" Buddy was trying to knock over a garbage can set out by the curb.

"No, Honey. I ain't. And I think we're runnin' outta time. They're getting ready for something a lot sooner than the new year. I been thinkin' about it, and I'm scared for you kids an' your mom. I don't think Ali'll want any witnesses hangin' around after he does whatever . . ."

"Dad, I've got an idea. Don't say no until you hear me out."

"OK, lemmie hear it."

"Promise you won't get mad and say no until you hear the whole thing?"

"Just tell me, Lynn."

"Well, you know I've made friends with AJ and Khristian?"

"That's the little Blondie with the camera, ain't it?"

"Yeah. Dad, they're so nice, the whole family. When I'm over there, they treat me like one of the family. And even though our boys are still brats to AJ and Khristian, they treat me great. I really like them. I like that whole family."

"That's great, Lynn. But it don't help us none. Buddy, stop it!" Charles jerked on the chain and pulled the dog back even with him and Lynn.

"Ali was afraid that Blondie had took his picture that night at her Halloween party. He didn't want to chance bein' recognized before they did whatever it was they're gonna do. But now, they told me to forget about it—getting the camera. So you don't need ta keep bein' friends with Blondie."

"Dad, you don't get it. I want to be friends with her. I like her, a lot. She talks too much, but she's really funny. And the whole family is so nice. Did you know her uncle works for the sheriff's department?"

"What! Why didn't cha tell me that before? That could be a problem for us."

"No, Dad. It could be the answer to our problems."

"Whadda ya mean?"

"Well, what if you talked to AJ's uncle? What if you told him how these guys are blackmailing you? Maybe, if you help the cops catch these guys before they hurt anyone, they won't press any charges against you. Dad, it's your chance to do the right thing."

"I jus' don't know, Lynn. I don't wanna go back ta jail."

"Dad, do you really think these guys are going to leave us as witnesses after they do whatever it is they're going to do? I think they plan to kill us, all of us. Think about it."

"I been thinking on it. How'd we do it? They never let the whole family leave the house at the same time. 'Specially now that they're so jittery. How could I meet with the cops without Ali findin out?"

Lynn was quiet while she thought about that. They reached the park and sat down at the picnic table, staring blankly at the pond. Buddy, for once, seemed content to lie quietly.

"Dad, I know what we can do. Let's talk a lot in front of those guys about how bad Buddy is, and how we need to train him to walk properly on a leash. You and I will make plans in front of them to walk Buddy every night, together. That'll give us an excuse for leaving the house every night."

"What good'll that do?"

"Well, it'll give us an excuse to get away from the house, and maybe we'll think of a way we can ask for help and still keep you out of trouble. At least we can talk to each other without one of them listening to us. Will you do it, Dad?"

"Sounds pretty complicated. What if we do decide to talk to Blondie's uncle and what if the cops won't give me a break?"

"Dad, I don't think we have a choice. Not if we want to save our family."

Lynn and Charles sat for a long time staring at the dark water, listening to the bullfrogs croaking. The weather had finally cooled off a little, and if it weren't for the heavy weight of decision hanging over them, it would have been great to just sit and enjoy the cool evening, a real rarity in Florida.

Finally, Charles said, "Let me think on it overnight."

"Dad, I love you. I know you'll do the right thing." Buddy jumped up just then and chased a duck right into the pond. Charles was so preoccupied; he'd loosened his hold on the leash.

They dragged the wet dog from the pond and started for home. Suddenly, Buddy stopped and vigorously shook the water from his body, soaking both Charles and Lynn. "Oh, well," Lynn said, "this'll make our story about needing to train this stupid mutt look more convincing."

As they walked home, Charles and Lynn decided they would make a big deal about how bad Buddy had acted tonight. They would pretend to come up with the idea of walking him every night for training. They also decided that the next night, Monday, they would take him for another walk and see what happened. If the men weren't suspicious, Tuesday they might try to have AJ get her uncle to come to the park so they could talk to him while they were out with Buddy.

What's Face Recognition Software?

Monday, when AJ got home from school, she rushed through her homework so that when Khristian called they could plan out what they were going to tell Uncle Eric about the paper.

When Khristian did call, he was very excited. "AJ this is great! Even better than I thought it would be. The requirements for this paper are research, an interview with an expert on the subject, a practical demonstration, and a written paper. If your Uncle Eric is willing to help me with all that, I know we can find out who those guys are. You do still have that photo we printed out with the close-up of Lynn's dad and those two men, don't you?"

"Yeah, I do. Maybe for the practical demonstration we can get them to run that photo through the face recognition software. We'll say that we know Lynn's dad was in jail, so he should show up when the photo's run through."

"I never thought of that. How are we going to get your uncle to take both of us to the sheriff's office?"

"I'll just tell him that I'm really interested in the face recognition software, too. I can say that I'm going to use the information for a paper at my school. He would be helping both of us.

"He should be home from work in a half hour. Why don't you call him and make the arrangements then?"

"I'll do that. My mom is really happy that I'm starting this paper early, and that I seem so interested in it. I almost feel guilty."

"Don't. You really are interested, and you really can write a paper on all of this. So you don't need to feel guilty."

AJ hung up the phone and went into her mom's bathroom where Max was sleeping in the shower. She woke him up and told him about the new plan to use the face recognition software.

"That's great," Max croaked.

"What's the matter with your voice?" AJ asked.

"I lost my voice because my allergies are acting up. That's why I couldn't talk yesterday when we were going to tell everyone what was going on. The medicine your mom gave me must be working. I'm feeling better and I've got my voice back. Well, kind of."

AJ hugged the big dog. "I'm glad you're OK. Last night, Khristian and I didn't know what had happened. We were so confused. We thought you'd decided not to talk in front of the adults after all."

"Well, if Khristian's plan works out, maybe I won't have to."

At the hellion children's house, Monday night went as planned by Lynn and Charles. No one seemed suspicious when they took Buddy for another walk. Saheb even made a joke, telling them to "Stay away from the duck pond."

The other men were way too engrossed in what they were doing in the back of the van to worry about what Lynn and Charles were doing with the dog. The only rule still enforced by the men was that the whole family could not leave the house at one time.

Late Tuesday afternoon, while the scruffy men were out working in the back of the van again, Lynn called AJ.

"AJ, I'm ready to tell you what's going on."

"That's great. Let's hear it."

"I can't talk on the phone, someone might hear me. Can you and Khristian meet me at the park at six o'clock tonight? My dad and I are going to pretend we're taking Buddy for a walk, you know, to leash train him. When we get there, my dad and I will tell you what's been going on."

"Oh no! We can't tonight. Khristian has swimming lessons, and I have piano. And tomorrow, my uncle is taking us to the sheriff's department to do research on papers we're writing. Can we meet you on Thursday?"

"It really needs to be tonight. Isn't there any way you can be there?"

"I'm sorry, but we can't. I have to go now; my mom's waiting in the car for me." AJ hung up the phone and ran out of the house.

"AJ . . . ," Lynn said, but she heard the phone disconnect. She went to tell her dad that they wouldn't be able to talk to AJ until Thursday.

"That's three more days," Charles said. "I hope it ain't too late to stop 'em."

"I'll try to get her to meet us tomorrow night and not wait until Thursday," Lynn said.

"Did you say Blondie's uncle is a sheriff's deputy?"

"Yeah, he is," Lynn answered. "Dad, don't you think we'd better go ahead and go for our walk with Buddy? You know, to make this look good for Thursday night."

Charles agreed, and they walked Buddy to the park and back without incident.

When AJ got home from piano lessons, she told Max about Lynn's phone call.

Max said, "I wish I could go over there and get into that garage. Then we would know exactly what those men are doing in the van."

"Max, I've got an idea. Can you sniff explosives, like those police dogs I saw on TV?"

"I don't know. I've never tried. But I'm sure we would have a much better chance of catching those guys with no one getting hurt if I could tell the police what's going on in that garage."

"Max, do you know what you just said? You said, 'if I could tell them.' Are you still thinking of letting the adults know you can talk?"

"If I thought it would help everyone be safe, I would. But I don't think it would make a difference at this point. It's probably still not a good idea to let the adults know I can talk."

"OK, let's go back to the kitchen and print another one of those photos of the men. I folded the other one, and I need to have a good copy when we go to see the face recognition software tomorrow."

"While you're doing that, why don't you let me out the front door? I'm going over there to see what's going on in that garage."

"Max, you can't. It's dangerous."

"It will be more dangerous for the police if they don't know exactly what's going on in that garage. Are you going to let me out or not?"

"I'll let you out, but please be careful. They keep all the garage doors shut and locked, and Sam is always standing guard. How are you going to get in?"

"I'm sure they'll have the windows open to get some air. It's pretty warm out tonight. If I can't get in the garage, I'll just listen under the window, like I did before."

AJ checked to make sure the adults wouldn't see her let Max out the front door. They were all on the screened in porch talking. She went to the front door and let Max out. "Please be careful. I love you, Max."

"I love you, too, AJ. I'll be careful. Just don't forget to let me back in."

"How long will you be gone?"

"Long enough to find out something useful, I hope."

AJ shut the door and went to the kitchen where she printed another copy of the photo. Then she went to her room and changed into her pajamas. Everyone was still on the porch, so she took the opportunity to call Khristian."

"What took so long? I thought you were going to call me earlier," Khristian complained.

"I got home from piano late. Mom made a couple of stops on the way home. Then Max and I were talking."

"AJ! I want to know what's going on."

"K, I'm worried. Max wanted to go over to Lynn's house to see if he could find out what's going on in the garage. I let him out the front door a while ago, and he's not back yet."

"I'm sure he's fine."

"Oh, I almost forgot. When I was leaving for piano, Lynn called. I didn't have time to talk to her because Mom was waiting in the car. Lynn said she wants to talk to us, both Lynn and her dad. They want to tell us what's going on. I told her I couldn't talk tonight. Can you come early tomorrow night so we can go over there before we go to the Sheriff's Department?"

"I'll try to get my mom to bring me over early, like around four."

After AJ and Khristian hung up, AJ ran to the front door to see if Max was back yet, but he wasn't.

At Lynn's house, Max was sniffing around the garage, trying to find a way in. When he could not, he settled down under an open window and hoped his super-sensitive ears would hear something worthwhile.

After about fifteen minutes, from inside the garage Max heard something metal hit the garage floor, then some language he didn't understand. But he understood from the tone of voice that it must be cursing.

"You idiot. Are you trying to kill all of us?"

"Please do not be yelling. It was an accident," Saheb said.

"That kind of accident can blow up this whole block. Be more careful."

Max had heard all he needed to hear. The terrorists were definitely working with explosives. Now the question was how to tell the authorities. Max went home and sat on the front porch, waiting for AJ to let him in.

"Max," AJ said when she opened the door, "what took you so long? I was getting worried. I've been sneaking out here every few minutes to see if you were back yet."

Max dashed in the door and led AJ to her room. She shut her door and flopped on her bed. Max jumped up next to her.

"For a long time, I didn't hear anything, just the sound of metal against metal, like tools being used. Then it sounded like someone dropped something, and one of the men said they had to be careful or they'd blow up the whole block. That has to mean it's explosives."

"Great! Now how do we let the police know? 'Hey! Everyone. Remember the other night when Khristian and I told you all that Max could talk? Well, he talked again last night and told us that some scruffy men have explosives in the garage at the hellion children's house.' What do you think, Max? Think they'll go for it?"

"I thought you didn't want us to call it the hellion children's house anymore." Max said. "Look, I know this is a problem. We lost some credibility the other night when I had laryngitis."

"Ya think? Some credibility? I don't think they'll ever believe us again."

"It's too late to worry about it now. Let's see what happens after you see the face recognition software tomorrow night."

The next day, AJ could hardly concentrate at school. As she rode her bike home, she kept pedaling faster and faster, wanting to get home and get on with it.

"I don't know why you were in such a hurry to get home," Max said when she arrived. "You're not leaving for the sheriff's office until six forty-five."

"I know. It's just that . . . I don't know. I guess I just want all this resolved. Besides, Khristian is going to try to come over early. We wanted to talk to Lynn again."

"Well, that'll give me some more time to think about everything that's happened."

"Like what?"

"Whether I should tell Uncle Bubbie what I heard. Then he could get the authorities involved and . . . and I don't know what. I'm confused, too. But I still think it would be a big mistake to let the adults know I can talk."

"Well, I might as well do my homework so I won't have to worry about it later. Hopefully, Khristian should be here soon."

When Khristian arrived, AJ and Max brought him up to date regarding the explosives. Max finished by restating his worry—how to let the adults know about the explosives without telling them he could talk.

The two kids and Max sat in silence for a few minutes.

"Hey! Wait a minute. I've got an idea," Khristian said.

"You seem to be the idea man, lately. Let's hear it," Max answered.

"I'm open to most anything," AJ added.

"What about your friend JJ?" Khristian said to Max.

"JJ? You mean the German shepherd living around the corner?"

"Yeah. Isn't he some kind of retired police dog?"

"Yes, he is. He worked for ATF."

"What's ATF?" AJ and Khristian asked at the same time.

"ATF stands for Alcohol, Tobacco and Firearms. JJ used to sniff out dope or explosives or something. I don't remember if he ever said which."

"Perfect!" Khristian shouted. "Can you get him to go over to the hellion children's house and see what he can sniff out?"

"Well, Khristian, that's not a bad idea at all. I'm almost sorry I bit you that day. The problem will be how to get him over to the hellion children's house. Dora and Frank pretty much keep him inside the fenced-in yard now."

"Let's go over there, right now. AJ, you ask Tia Dora if we can take JJ for a walk with Max. Do you think she'll go for it?" Dora and Frank were from Brazil, and Tia was Spanish for aunt. When Dora's niece Regina was staying with her last summer, she, AJ and Khristian had been great friends. Regina was teaching AJ and Khristian to speak Spanish, and AJ and Khristian had taken to calling Mrs. Johnson Tia Dora, like Regina did.

"She might. We used to walk JJ and Max together all the time."

"Great idea," Max said. "It'll be good to see old JJ again."

AJ, Khristian, and Max set out for the Johnson's house. When they rang the doorbell, Dora came to the door.

"AJ, Khristian, it's so good to see you." She gave each child a hug. "You should come visit me more often, even though Regina is gone now. I miss seeing you kids. Hi, Max," she added as she patted his head.

"Tia Dora, we were wondering, would you like for us to take JJ for a walk? We haven't done that since Regina went back to Brazil. We thought he might be lonely for Max."

"That would be wonderful. I think he misses you kids. Let me get him, he's out back."

A few minutes later, Dora came back into the living room. JJ was on a leash, and he was wearing a muzzle. He rushed up to the kids and Max. He was so excited to see them, he was whining.

"Why is he wearing a muzzle?" Khristian asked.

"Well, those kids that live across the street at the loco house said JJ is vicious. That girl, Royanne, accused JJ of biting her. She didn't have a mark on her, but they threatened to sue us. So now when we take JJ for a walk, we put the muzzle on him."

"Oh, Tia Dora, that's awful. Poor JJ." AJ knelt next to the German shepherd and hugged his neck. "You wouldn't hurt anyone, would you, Boy?" JJ whined and nuzzled AJ's hand.

"But he would," Dora said. "He would hurt someone if he knew they were a criminal. Like if they had illegal drugs or explosives. That's what he did for years when he was a police dog. But he's never hurt anyone who didn't deserve it. And now, he's retired and I've never even heard him growl at anyone," Dora said. "It's so sad that loco Royanne caused all this trouble."

Khristian took JJ's leash, and AJ grabbed Max's.

"If you see any of those kids from the loco house, stay far away from them with JJ," Tia Dora said.

After the door shut, Khristian said, "This is a great neighborhood. You've got the hellion children's house, the loco lady, and her family."

"Hey! Don't knock my neighborhood," AJ said. "You're always plenty anxious to come over here."

"That's because it's so exciting. There's never a dull minute," Khristian said. "Let's take the dogs to the park, and Max can fill JJ in on what's happening."

"Do you think JJ will shun Max for talking to us?" Khristian whispered to AJ.

"I don't know. Since he was a police dog, he must care a lot about what happens to us humans. Maybe he'll understand."

When they reached the park, the kids sat at the picnic table, facing toward the pond. The dogs sat in front of them.

"Well . . . ," Khristian said.

"Well . . . now what?" AJ said.

"Look, JJ, we need your help," Khristian started. "We know you're retired and all that, but we think there are some very bad men in the neighborhood, and we're afraid that if we don't do something to stop them; people might get hurt."

JJ cocked his head as he sat staring intently at the kids. When Khristian finished, JJ laid his head on Khristian's lap and whined.

"See, he understands," Khristian said to AJ. "You understand, don't cha, Boy?"

"So now what do we do?" AJ asked.

"Good question. Max, you got any ideas?"

"Why don't you two walk down to the pond and give us some privacy. Let us know if you see anyone coming."

The little park was a very popular place in the neighborhood. There were always people there feeding the ducks or taking walks around the small lake.

AJ and Khristian walked down to the edge of the water.

Max explained everything that had happened so far and asked JJ for his help. Then he sat there waiting for JJ to respond.

"Hermmmphf!"

"What did you say?" Max asked.

"Hermmphf," JJ said again.

"I don't speak German. Can you translate?" Max asked.

"Hermmphf," JJ pawed the muzzle, and Max finally got it.

"Oh, you can't talk with that thing on. These things should be outlawed. They're cruel and unusual punishment."

"Hermmphf," JJ pawed the muzzle again.

"You agree, huh," Max said.

The German shepherd walked over to Max and butted him with his head. Then he pawed the muzzle again.

"Oh, you want it off. Wait here, I'll get the kids." Max walked down to the water's edge.

"Is he going to help us?" Khristian asked.

"I don't know. With that muzzle on, I can't understand a word he's saying."

"We should have thought of that," AJ said. "Let's go take it off of him. I hate those things, anyway."

"Wait," Khristian said. "What if Royanne comes by while we have the muzzle off of JJ? She'll sue Tia Dora."

"We'll just have to keep watch and put it back on if we see her coming," AJ said as she pulled the Velcro straps loose on the muzzle. Once she had it off of JJ, she scratched his nose for him. "I bet that feels great, huh, Boy?"

"You two need to go back down to the pond. I can't talk to JJ with you here."

Once the kids were out of hearing distance, JJ said, "So, Max, you broke the Animal Code of Silence. This must be very serious."

"It is, JJ, or I would never have broken the code. Are you going to shun me?"

"Well, you're not the first animal to speak to humans, and I doubt you'll be the last. Remember Balaam's donkey?"

"Sure, all the animals have heard that bible story. This is a little different, though. It's not the Master trying to communicate with a human who won't listen. This time, I overheard a conversation, and I knew the kids were in danger. I couldn't think of any other way to keep them safe. I had to warn them."

"Those scruffy men sure sound like bad news. Let me get this straight. Last night you heard something about explosives?"

"Yeah. Somebody dropped something, and one of the men said they could have blown up the whole block."

"Well, let's go to the hellion children's house. I need to get up close to that garage—inside if possible. I'll see if I can sniff anything out. If it's enough explosives to blow up a whole block, it should be a pretty strong scent, even for my old nose."

Max called AJ and Khristian back from the pond's edge and told them what needed to be done. AJ said, "I'm sorry, JJ. But I think I have to put this stupid muzzle back on you. I don't want Tia Dora getting into trouble if you don't have it on." JJ walked over to AJ and sat still, waiting for her to reattach the hated muzzle.

"I'm putting it on very loosely. I don't want it to interfere with your nose."

Once the muzzle was back in place, AJ and Khristian reattached JJ and Max's leashes and started for the hellion children's house.

"It would help if we could get Lynn to talk to us," AJ said.

"Hey, AJ! Do you realize you and JJ, a dog, have almost the same name?" Khristian asked."

"Don't start. My name is my initials used as a nickname. I don't know where JJ got his name."

"I hope we don't run into Lynn's brothers. I can't stand those guys."

"Me either. They are so wild. Last night we heard noise outside at eleven o'clock, and all three of her brothers were outside, playing with their skateboards. At eleven o'clock on a school night!"

"How are we going to find out what's going on in that garage if they don't go to bed soon? Our parents aren't going to let us stay out after eleven o'clock at night."

"Tell me about it. My curfew is dark."

"Mine, too."

The kids slowed down as they neared Lynn's house. The boys were nowhere in sight, but they could be hiding around any corner, just waiting to attack.

Khristian said, "Why don't you go see if Lynn wants to take Buddy for another walk with us. That'll give us an excuse to go up to the house. While you're at the front door, I'll try to get JJ close to the garage."

"OK, but be careful. I can see that guy Sam standing just inside the door."

"Don't worry. I'm too scared not to be careful—of the scruffy guys and those brothers of Lynn's."

AJ knocked on the door and Lynn answered.

"I know I told you that we were busy tonight, but we don't have to leave until six forty-five. Do you want to take Buddy for a short walk? He could use the practice on a leash and you can tell us what's bothering you."

"I can't. My mom and dad aren't here now so I can't go anywhere until they get back. What's Khristian doing with JJ? I heard that dog was dangerous."

"No, he's not dangerous. He's a great dog. Royanne was just causing trouble, as usual. I think it runs in her family."

"What—craziness?"

"No, trouble making."

Just then, JJ went into a frenzy. He started whining and digging at the bottom of the wooden access door to the garage.

"Why are Max and JJ sniffing around the garage? Get them away from there, AJ. If those guys see them, we'll all be in trouble."

"Lynn, please, tell us what's going on."

"I will, but I need time to explain. My dad's gone and I can't leave the house. We'll talk tomorrow. You will be able to talk tomorrow, won't you?"

"I think so," AJ answered.

"I'm pretty sure my dad is going to come with me, to explain how this started. Can you bring your uncle, the one who's a cop?"

"Probably, but why?"

Lynn whispered, "AJ, this is very serious. My dad . . . look, just bring your uncle, OK? And bring Max. Make it look like you and your uncle are just walking the dog. My dad and I are going to pretend we're walking Buddy."

"OK, if that's what you want. We should probably get JJ home and go meet my uncle now. I'll ask him when he picks us up. We'll see you tomorrow night. At the park."

"Please, get that dog away from the garage." Lynn went over and helped Khristian pull JJ across the driveway and out to the street. JJ was very agitated.

When AJ and Max joined Khristian and JJ on the street, AJ bent over to pretend she was adjusting JJ's muzzle. What she actually did was loosen it all the way, so he and Max could talk, or whatever it was dogs did to communicate. "OK, you two. Talk fast. We have to get JJ back home and go meet Uncle Eric."

"Khristian, Lynn wants me to bring my Uncle Eric to the park tomorrow night. She said her dad wants to talk to him. I wonder what that's all about."

"Man, I wish I could be there. Do you think your uncle will go?"

"I'm pretty sure he will, unless he has to work or something."

When they reached Tia Dora's house, she was waiting on the porch for them, and thanked them for walking JJ. The kids started for home. They wanted to ask Max what JJ had told him, but they couldn't. There were too many people out in their yards and walking on the street. Both kids were dying of curiosity.

As they turned the corner, they saw Uncle Eric was waiting to take them to the sheriff's department, so they still didn't get a chance to talk to Max. Uncle Eric started yelling at the kids, telling them to hurry up or they were going to be late. He was really mad. AJ forgot all about asking Uncle Eric to go to the park the following night.

Driving into the parking lot at the county complex, Uncle Eric was full of instructions.

"Stay with me at all times. We'll have to go through the booking area to get to the IT department, so if anyone is causing a ruckus or anything, stay right behind me. Don't look at any of the prisoners. Don't talk to anyone unless I introduce you to them. You two got all that?"

"Yes," both Khristian and AJ said meekly. They felt overwhelmed.

While they were waiting in the lobby for Uncle Eric to sign them in and get temporary badges, AJ opened her notebook and pulled out the fresh copy of the photo she had printed.

"That looks good," Khristian said. "Did you mess with the photo program anymore?"

"I just increased the pixels. Listen to me; I'm starting to sound like a computer nerd like you."

"I am *not* a computer nerd."

"Are too."

"Am not!"

"Stop it, you two. This isn't the time for one of your arguments. We have to wait here in the lobby for a few minutes for Mike from the IT department to come get us. Why don't you sit down over there?" Eric indicated a couple of chairs across the room. "I'm just going to run up to my locker and get something I forgot. I'll be right back. *Don't move*."

"Jeez! We won't," AJ said.

"What's he so uptight about?" Khristian asked.

"You got me. Must be this place. It sure gives me the creeps."

Khristian and AJ waited for about five minutes before Uncle Eric returned. He was with another guy who was really tall. He must have been six-six. Next to Uncle Eric, who was only five-ten, the guy looked like a giant.

"Mike, this is my niece, AJ, and her friend Khristian. AJ and Khristian, this is Mike Rose, our resident computer geek."

"Hey!" Mike said. "I resemble that remark. Hi, kids."

After the introductions, Mike told everyone to follow him and he would take them to the IT area of the sheriff's department. "We're going to walk through the booking area, then the communications center, so you'll need to be very quiet."

AJ and Khristian didn't mutter a sound. They were both wide-eyed taking in all the action. When they went through the booking area, there were two sheriff's deputies wrestling a guy who must have weighed 300 pounds to the ground, trying to get handcuffs on him. Eric grabbed the two kids and pulled them away from the scuffle.

"Do they make handcuffs that big?" Khristian asked. But no one answered him.

The communications center was dark, with the computer monitors providing the only light in the room. There was a low hum of background noise, and the kids could actually hear deputies in patrol cars talking to each other and to the dispatchers. They heard a noise like a siren, and Mike explained softly that the sound was the ring of the nine-one-one emergency line.

At the far end of the communications center they passed through yet another steel door into a room that was a real mess. There were computers, monitors, and printers everywhere, wires snaked in every direction, and every surface seemed to be covered with the litter of half-full coffee cups, soda cans, pizza boxes, and sandwich wrappers.

"We're not a very neat bunch," Mike said.

Eric gave the kids a look that warned them not to comment on the mess.

"So, you're writing papers on the face recognition software we use. I can't believe your teacher is letting you both write on the same subject."

"Oh, we don't go to the same school. Khristian is home-schooled, and I go to St. Mark's," AJ answered.

"OK, get your writing pads out. I'm going to give you a little background first."

The kids did as they were told, and Mike continued.

"Tampa, Florida, was the first city in the United States to install face recognition software. It was first used for the 2001 Super Bowl. Because of what happened on Nine-Eleven, authorities were trying to find a way to keep people safer at large events where lots of people would be attending. Unfortunately, there are a lot of critics of face recognition software, and they started calling the 2001 Super Bowl the 'Snooper Bowl'."

"Why don't they like the idea of the cameras and software?" AJ asked.

"Some people feel that it's an infringement on their freedoms. My view is, if you're not doing anything wrong, you don't have anything to worry about."

"Who makes the software?" Khristian asked.

"The software in Tampa comes from a company called Visionics Corp. After the Super Bowl, they offered the city a free trial of the face recognition program called Face-It. Thirty-six cameras were installed in the Ybor City entertainment district."

"How are those cameras monitored?"

"They were monitored by a Tampa police officer in a room about three blocks away from Ybor City. I can't disclose the exact location. From there, the officer could click a mouse and scan a face from the crowd to download to a criminal database to search for matches. The Ybor City program wasn't real successful, so it was discontinued."

"Why is that?"

"Well, people visiting Ybor City are unconstrained. At the Super Bowl, the crowd was funneled through gates and doorways. They had to stop to show their tickets. The cameras could be mounted at eye level, and there were even flashing lights or noises that would cause people to look up—kind of like tricking them into posing for the cameras. That way, most of the pictures were full face shots.

"But as I said, in Ybor city, people were free to move wherever and however they wished. The cameras were mounted high on light poles on the streets, and the crowd could walk slowly or fast, which might blur the pictures. They could walk close to the buildings or out near the streets. It was hard to get a picture at an optimal angle for the software to work with."

"I can see where that would be a problem," AJ said.

Mike continued, "One night, a bunch of people who weren't happy with the whole camera thing, put on head scarves, hats, masks and even those Groucho Marx glasses with the plastic nose and moustache. They just marched up and down the streets in Ybor City dancing and making rude gestures to the cameras."

AJ and Khristian giggled. "Are there cameras installed anywhere else?" Khristian asked.

"There are cameras at Tampa International Airport and here at the county complex at the jail and jail visitation center. You'd be surprised how many wanted criminals come to visit their friends who are in jail."

"Can we see an actual demonstration of how the software works?" AJ asked.

"Sure we'll get to that in just a minute. Do you have any other questions about anything we've already covered? If not, I have some printed information from the companies who make the software that I'll give you when you leave."

"I have one question," AJ said. "What if a citizen had a picture of someone, maybe someone in his neighborhood that he thought might be a criminal? Can you scan in photos and run them against your database?"

"Sure. We do that right over here." Mike walked across the room to a flatbed scanner. We scan the photo in here. Then we pull it up on this screen and tell the system which databases we want to scan."

"I brought a picture with me," AJ said. "We have a neighbor who's been in jail. If we scan this picture of him into the database, will he show up?"

"I don't know," Mike said. "But that would be a good practical demonstration for you. Give me the picture."

AJ opened her notebook and took out the photo. Mike laid it on the glass and scanned it into the system. Then he pulled the picture up on the monitor. "There are three guys here. Which one is the guy who was in jail?"

AJ pointed out Charles. Mike used the mouse to draw a circle around Charles's face and enlarge it on the screen. While he was working, Khristian pulled AJ back a couple of steps.

"We need him to try to match one of those other guys. How can we get him to do that?"

"Ask, I guess," AJ whispered. Aloud, she said, "Mike, could we possibly have the system look at all three of the faces in the photo? To see if it picks Charles out of the three?"

"AJ, you're really pushing it," Uncle Eric said.

"No, Eric, I'm glad they're interested, and it would be a good demonstration of this part of the system. OK, kids. I'm going to tell the system to search on all three faces in the photo."

AJ made a face at Uncle Eric's back. He sure was being a pain. Khristian laughed and Eric gave him a dirty look.

"It takes a long time to try to match a face, and it will take longer to look at all three faces. While the system is processing, let me show you where we monitor the people coming into the county complex."

They walked with Mike and Eric to the other end of the room, where they learned a lot more about how face recognition software works, more than enough to write a paper. After about forty-five minutes, Mike said, "That about wraps it up. Let's go see if the system found matches for any of the faces in the photo we scanned in."

"Well, look at this. We have a hit!" Mike said.

"Who is it?" Uncle Eric asked. "The guy who was in jail?"

"No, it's one of the other faces. See here, this guy who's standing behind the guy who answered the door. It says he's Ali Ben Hakeem, wanted in connection with a suspected terrorist cell."

"A terrorist, I knew it!" AJ yelped.

"Don't get too excited, AJ," Mike said. "Unfortunately, the system comes up with a lot of false-positives."

"What does that mean?" Khristian asked.

"Well, face recognition isn't an exact science. The human face has so many planes and angles; it's difficult for software to digitize it. Did any of you read in the newspapers about the guy from Tampa who was eating lunch in Ybor City and had his photo taken by one of the cameras there? Somehow the photo was blown up and used in the company's marketing literature. A copy was printed in a national magazine and some lady from out west called the Tampa police and said this guy was wanted for child endangerment or child neglect, something like that.

"Anyway, when the cops went to arrest the guy at his job here in Tampa, they found out it was the wrong guy."

"Wow! What happened?"

"Let's just say he wasn't too happy. That incident caused the ACLU to get involved with our whole face recognition program. So now, we don't jump to conclusions. We do a lot of investigating before we go to arrest anyone who pulls a hit from the software."

"So what happens now?" Eric asked.

"Let's go find a conference room where we can talk about that," Mike said.

On the way to the conference room, Mike and Uncle Eric got some coffee and bought AJ a soda. Khristian had given up soda for his New Year's resolution last January, so he had some juice. After they got their drinks, Mike took them into a small conference room, where they all sat around a big table.

Mike laid the photo AJ had given him, along with the report from the database on the table. "What can you kids tell us about this guy?"

"About him specifically, nothing really. But there have been a lot of strange things going on in our neighborhood."

"Like what?"

"Well, remember that I told you that a man in our neighborhood was recently released from jail? I think that was in the middle of the summer. I'm not sure, because I was gone to visit my dad in Austin, Texas.

"Anyway, not long after he got out of jail, three guys came to stay at his house, and that guy is one of them."

"What else?"

"Well, the night of my Halloween party, we had a scavenger hunt. I was on the team that went to the hellion children's house?"

"What's the hellion children's house?"

"We just call it that because the kids who live there are so mean. My grandma calls them little hellions. Except for my friend Lynn."

"I'm getting confused."

"Maybe I can help," Uncle Eric said. "According to AJ, the guy who just got out of jail is the dad of the hellion children. The night of AJ's Halloween party, I was one of the chaperones. We went to their house to try to get some items from our list, for the scavenger hunt, you know?"

"Anyway, when the guy opened the door . . ."

"Which guy?"

"The one who was in jail. He's the owner of the house. The bratty boys are his kids. Anyway, he opened the door and screamed for us to get off of his property. Two other guys were standing behind him. That's when AJ took that picture we scanned into the face recognition database."

"OK, but what was so strange about that? It just sounds like a cranky neighbor to me."

"Uncle Eric, we had Max with us, remember? He started barking and growling at those men. He was really upset. It wasn't like him."

"Who's Max?" Mike asked.

"Max is AJ's dog. And she's right. He doesn't get upset, especially not like he did that night, not without good reason."

"Great. The kid's dog got upset. Eric, we can't take that to the captain. Isn't there anything else?"

"Tell them about Lynn trying to be your friend," Khristian said to AJ.

"The next day, Khristian and I were walking Max. When we went past the hellion children's house, the daughter, Lynn, invited Khristian and me for a swim."

"Oh, that's really strange," Mike said sarcastically. "Come on, there must be something else." Mike was getting exasperated.

"You don't understand. None of the kids from that house have ever had anything to do with me. They are really mean. They call me a goody-two-shoes. Sometimes they throw rocks at us. They always make fun of us. Then the day after the Halloween party, all of a sudden, Lynn invites us for a swim at their house."

"Is this going anywhere?" Mike asked.

"When AJ and I went over there, we took Max with us. Max got all upset again, running around, barking and growling. We had to leave and take him home," Khristian explained. "Max isn't a mean dog. There has to be someone at that house he doesn't like."

"Eric," Mike said, "just because the dog got upset doesn't mean anything. At least not anything we can take to the captain."

"Wait, there's more," AJ interrupted.

"What?" both Mike and Eric said at the same time.

"We invited Lynn over for dinner. When we left the room, she was searching through my stuff for my camera. I think she was going to take it because of that picture."

"What makes you think that?" Mike said.

"It's just a feeling I got," AJ said sheepishly. She couldn't tell the two men that Max had seen her searching and told AJ and Khristian.

"Well, I'm afraid I can't take your feelings to the captain either," Mike said.

"Wait," Khristian said. "Tonight AJ and I were walking Max, and we were also walking JJ. JJ's a retired police dog that was adopted by a family in AJ's neighborhood. He used to be in some drug department, I can't remember the name, but the dogs sniffed out drugs and explosives and stuff."

"ATF?" Mike asked.

"Yeah, that's it. Anyway, we went over to the hellion children's house, and while AJ was talking to Lynn, I went over by the garage. Those guys in the picture were in there with the doors all shut up. JJ started whining and digging at the door, trying to get into the garage. Maybe he smelled drugs or explosives."

"Great. Now we've got the testimony of two kids and two dogs who don't like these neighbors," Mike said.

AJ jumped up, "Khristian, we forgot to tell them the most important part—what Lynn asked me to do tonight."

"What was that?" Uncle Eric said.

"Lynn is the sister from the hellion children's house. She and Khristian and I have become friends. But she's been really upset lately. We asked her if it was because of those scruffy men at her house, and she started crying. Then she said that she really needs to tell us why she's upset, because if she doesn't tell us, people could get hurt. But if she does tell us, then her family could get hurt. She asked me to bring Uncle Eric to meet her and her dad at the little park in our neighborhood tomorrow night."

"Why didn't you tell me this before?" Uncle Eric exploded.

"We didn't have a chance. As soon as we got home tonight, you wanted to leave, then you had all those rules for us, and then . . ." AJ had tears in her eyes.

"AJ, calm down. It's OK. I know I'm too impatient sometimes." Eric walked over to AJ's chair and gave her a hug.

"OK," Mike said, "that's more like it. I think we have good reason to bring the captain in."

"Look, Mike. It's getting late, and I need to take these kids home. Why don't you take what we've got to the captain? I'll be back in about an hour, after I get these two home. We'll see what he wants to do about tomorrow night."

"There's something else," AJ said. "Lynn said that tomorrow night, Uncle Eric and I should pretend that we're just taking Max for a walk, not like we're going to meet them. I guess she doesn't want those men to get suspicious."

"You're not going anywhere near that park," Eric said.

Mike said, "Eric, take the kids home and come back. We'll talk about how to handle tomorrow night after we talk to the captain."

On the way home, Uncle Eric kept telling AJ and Khristian that they couldn't talk about what had just happened, not even to their parents. He said he would brief the parents after he met with his captain, but probably not until tomorrow night or maybe even Friday. He also repeated how important it was that whenever the kids thought anyone was in danger, they let an adult know what was going on right away.

It was after nine o'clock when they dropped Khristian at home. He opened the door and leaned back in to grab his notebook. He whispered to AJ, "I know I'm not going to be allowed to use the phone this late. I'll call you tomorrow, when you get home from school."

At home, when AJ was finally in bed, Max came in and jumped up on the bed to talk to her. He missed the top of the bed the first time and had to try again.

"Max, you need more exercise. Did you hurt yourself?"

"No, I just can't get used to your new bed. It sits up too high."

"I don't think it's that high. I think you just can't jump like you used to. You're getting old."

"Do I have to give you the lecture about respecting your elders?"

"No, please don't."

"What happened tonight?"

"Max, I have so much to tell you," AJ said. Then she described to him in detail everything that had happened at the sheriff's department. "Oh, I almost forgot. What about JJ? Did he sniff out anything?"

"Yes," Max said, "He confirmed that there are explosives in that garage, probably a lot of them. He said the scent was very strong."

"I don't think I'll be able to sleep tonight knowing that. Do you think I should tell Uncle Eric and Mike?"

"What proof do you have, except a talking dog?"

"I see your point. Are you going to sleep in here tonight?"

"No. If I did, that stupid cat would be right up here bugging me. I'll be in the shower."

"Night, Max."

"Goodnight, Alyssa."

The phone was ringing when AJ walked in from school the next afternoon. Of course it was Khristian.

"Did you tell your mom and dad?" AJ asked him.

"Are you kidding? I'm going to let your Uncle Eric or your mom do that. Mom would flip out if I tried to explain all this."

"Yeah, I know what you mean. I wonder when Eric will tell my mom and grandparents. Hang on, the other line is ringing." AJ put Khristian on hold and answered the other line. It was Uncle Eric.

"AJ, I'll be over at about six o'clock. You and I will take Max for a walk and meet Charles and Lynn at the park."

"What are you going to tell my mom, and Mema and Papa?"

"We can't tell them anything yet. I'll just say I stopped by for a few minutes. You can ask me to go for a walk with you and Max. OK?"

"OK. But I'm sure they're going to wonder why you and I are taking Max for a walk."

"Let's just do what I said, and we'll see what happens."

"OK, see you later."

AJ went back to her call with Khristian. "Mr. K, are you still there?"

"I'm here. Was that Uncle Bubbie?"

"That sounds weird coming from you. Yeah, it was him."

"Well, do you get to go with him tonight?"

"Yes, I do. I'll call you when we get back and tell you what happens."

AJ hung up and went to the screened-in porch to let Max in.

"Max, Uncle Eric just called. You and I are going to the park with him tonight to talk to Lynn and her dad."

"I bet that makes you happy, Miss Nosy Rosy. Now you'll know what's going on. What's he going to tell Mema and Papa and your mom?"

"He said he can't tell them anything yet. He has to see what happens tonight. I sure hope Buddy doesn't go for another swim in the pond."

A couple of hours later, Uncle Eric pulled into the driveway.

"Hi. What are you doing here?" AJ's mom said when he came into the house.

"Oh, I was in the neighborhood and I thought I'd stop by and say hello. Where is everyone?"

"AJ's in her room, and Mom and Dad had some meeting at the church."

AJ came into the room with Max's leash in her hands. "Uncle Bubbie, will you go with me to take Max for a walk? It's almost dark, and I don't want to go by myself."

Eric acted surprised, "Well, I guess I could. How far are you going?"

"Just down to the park by the pond. It's not far."

"Okay, I'll go with you."

Amy said, "Maybe by the time you get back Mom and Dad will be home." Eric was glad she didn't offer to go with them.

As they reached the end of the driveway, AJ asked, "Well, did I do OK?"

"You did great. You haven't talked about this to anyone, have you?"

"Just Khristian, since he already knew about it."

"He didn't say anything to anyone, did he?"

"No. I think he's afraid of you."

"You should be afraid of me, too."

"Oh, I am. Can't you tell?" AJ laughed.

Help!

When AJ and Eric reached the park, Charles and Lynn weren't there yet. They sat on the picnic table bench to wait.

After about fifteen minutes, AJ said, "Do you think maybe the scruffy men wouldn't let them come?"

"I have no idea," Eric answered.

After another five minutes, Buddy came running into the park, dragging Charles and Lynn behind him. He ran straight to Max and tried to get him to play. Uncle Eric grabbed the pup's collar and pulled him away from Max.

AJ introduced Lynn and Charles to Uncle Eric.

"AJ told me that your daughter, Lynn, wanted me to meet you two here tonight. What did you want to talk to me about?" Eric asked.

"I don't really know where to start," Charles said.

"How about at the beginning," Uncle Eric said.

Duh! AJ thought.

Charles told Eric about his time in prison and having Saheb as his cellmate. He described how they became friends and shared things they'd done in the past, some of which the police didn't know about.

"I really don't wanna go back ta jail. I gotta decent job, and my family needs me. But Saheb tol his cousin, Ali, about some of the things I done, and now Ali's blackmailin' me."

"What have you done that's so bad that this guy, what's his name? Ali? That Ali can blackmail you?"

"Well, it's not that what I done is so bad, but I'm on parole. If I got arrested for any of that stuff, chances are good I'd be goin' back ta jail. But that's not the worst problem."

"What could be worse?" Uncle Eric sounded confused. AJ was listening intently.

"Well, Sahib, Ali and another guy have been stayin' at my house. I think they're part of some kind of terrorist cell or something."

At this, Uncle Eric sat up straighter on the bench. "What makes you think that?" he asked.

"Just let me tell ya my story. Then you can ask questions, and I promise, I'll answer em."

Charles went on. "At first, everything was friendly. It was just a couple of guys needin' a place to stay for a while. I'd done tol' Saheb he could stay with me, and even though it would crowd my family ta have two more guys there, I said they could stay for a few weeks while they got on their feet. I was feelin' pretty fortunate to have a home to go to when I got out of jail.

"Then, 'bout as soon as them men got moved in, they tol' me they'd need ta stay 'til after the first of the year. When I tol' em, they'd be overstayin' their welcome, they threatened ta tell the police about the things I'd tol' Saheb when we was in prison. I wasn't happy about it, but I tol' em they could stay.

"Then the night of little Blondie's Halloween party, things come to a head. I found a suspicious email message on my computer for Ali. We was arguin' 'bout it when you and the kids come to the door on that scavenger hunt. Blondie had a camera and was takin' pictures, and them guys was terrified that someone would see their pictures and recognize em. Seems they have some big doings comin' up, and they couldn't let that happen.

"From that night on, my family ain't been allowed to leave the house all at once. They sent me an' Saheb to try to steal the camera from Blondie. But we couldn't get inta the house because of that there dog barkin'." He pointed to Max.

AJ bent over and hugged Max. "Good boy, Max. You stopped them." She pushed Buddy away from the old dog. Buddy kept nipping at Max's back and paws trying to get him to play, but Max just snarled and ignored the pup.

Charles went on, "Then they made my girl, Lynn, promise she'd get Blondie's camera, or they'd hurt one of us."

AJ gasped, "Oh, no."

"Don't blame her, Blondie," Charles said, "they tol' her they'd hurt one of us iffen she didn't do what they said."

"I'm sorry, AJ. I didn't know you then, and I was so scared they would hurt my mom or dad. I'm so ashamed," Lynn said.

"Lynn, I forgive you. I know you must have been terrified."

Uncle Eric looked very angry. He stood up and pointed his finger at Charles. "Wait just a minute. Are you saying you tried to break into my parent's house and steal my niece's camera? And then when that didn't work, you sent your daughter to try to steal it?"

"Ya don' understand. I had ta. They threatened ta hurt my family. When we couldn't get the camera that night, they made Lynn come over there ta make friends with little Blondie and try ta get it. Lynn even went on that there church re-treat with the kids hopin' ta get the camera, but I guess you'd taken it on vacation."

"What? I didn't take AJ's camera on vacation. I have my own camera."

"Then why'd she tell Lynn you took it with you?"

Uh Oh! Max thought. *How do we explain how AJ and Khristian knew to be suspicious of Lynn?*

"I can explain that," AJ piped up.

Good, I'm glad someone can, Max thought.

"The night that Lynn came over to have supper with us, I thought she'd gone through my things looking for something." Lynn hung her head at this. "So when she asked about my camera, I told her yours was broken so you took mine with you on your vacation. I was trying to get enough time to find out what was going on. Khristian and I talked about it and decided that was the best thing to do."

"You knew I went through your stuff, and you were still nice to me?" Lynn said in awe.

"I thought you must have had a good reason," AJ improvised. Max was thinking, *Don't say anything else AJ. You talk way too much.* As if she'd heard his thoughts, AJ sat back quietly to see what would happen next.

"Well," Uncle Eric said, "what happened next?"

"Ali'd got to thinking maybe they couldn't wait 'til after the first of the year. I think the plan was to cause some kind of disturbance at the Outback Bowl over in Tampa on New Year's Day. I think it was supposed to be like—coordinated with some of them other people they been emailin' to. For a while there, I thought they decided they'd have to do something quicker and then get out of town fast. I ain't overheard nothin recently, but I think maybe they picked a new target."

"And . . . ," Eric was looking very, very cop-like.

"And . . . that's all I know. Look, I don't want nobody ta get hurt, but I'm afraid for my family. I love Lynn and my wife. And I love them boys of mine, even though they're little hellions."

At this AJ's head jerked up to look at Max, who gave her a wink. *Can dogs wink?*

"Can you help us?" Charles added.

"I'll do everything I can. I can't make any promises about you staying out of jail. I have no authority about that. But I will put in a good word for you. We need to think about how we're going to stop these guys. Do you know what kind of disturbance they're planning?"

"I sure don't. They bin out in my garage workin' in the back of my old van. None of us're allowed out there. I'm afraid they might be fixin' some kinda explosives or somethin'."

Charles continued, "We're gonna have to get back soon. We're just supposed to be walkin' the dog. You know, trainin' him to walk on a leash."

Uncle Eric said, "Can you get out again tomorrow night?"

"I think so. We made a big deal about havin' to train Buddy."

"Great. We'll meet again tomorrow night," Eric said, then looked around the park. There were several families walking their dogs. "This park might be too busy to talk privately. Why don't you two act like you're taking Buddy for a walk and stop at my mom and dad's house? We can have more privacy there. I have to talk to my boss, and probably the sheriff, and I really think we're probably going to have to get the FBI or Homeland Security involved. This is a very big deal." Eric was planning out loud.

After Lynn and her dad left, Uncle Eric just sat for a few minutes, thinking about everything that had been said. For once, AJ was quiet.

"AJ, I don't want you to go over there again. It's too dangerous."

"But Lynn is my friend. Besides, I always take Max with me."

"Yeah, like he'd be any protection."

You'd be surprised, AJ thought.

"I mean it, AJ. Do not go over there. And you have to keep quiet about this. I know how much you like to talk, but you can't breathe a word about this to anyone.

"Now, let's go home. I need to tell Mema, Papa, and your mom what's going on. After that, I have to go back to the sheriff's department and bring my boss up to date."

Later, when Uncle Eric finished telling the rest of the family what Charles had told him, they were astonished.

"I can't believe I let you and Khristian go over there," AJ's mom said.

"We were fine. We had Max with us," AJ answered.

"Yeah, like he'd be any protection," her mom said.

Hey! My feelings are getting hurt, Max thought.

While AJ's family discussed what Uncle Eric was going to do next, AJ and Max went into her room so she could call Khristian.

"No one seems to think you're much of a guard dog, Max"

"I got that idea. Why don't they think I can protect you?"

"Maybe it's because you're always so lazy."

"I'm not lazy. I'm just conserving my energy for when I really need it."

AJ punched in Khristian's number. When he answered, she told him what was going on.

"Man, I wish I could have been there. Do they really think those guys might be terrorists?"

"From what Lynn's dad said, it sounds like that's what he thinks. It was kind of hairy when I had to explain how we knew Lynn was trying to take my camera—film—whatever."

"How did you do that without telling them that Max told us?"

"I just said I could tell someone had been going through my things. Lynn was pretty embarrassed."

"She should be."

"Khristian, they made her do it. They threatened to hurt her family."

"Well, I guess that's different. What happens next?"

"I don't know. My uncle has to go back to the sheriff's department tonight and I suppose we won't know anything else until tomorrow night."

"Are you going to walk the dogs again tomorrow?"

"Uncle Eric thought the park might be too crowded. There were a lot of people there tonight. So he told Lynn and her dad to pretend they were walking the dog and come to my house."

"Cool! Maybe I can come over?"

"I doubt that my mom will say yes with all this stuff going on."

"Well, call me and keep me informed."

AJ promised that she would. The kids said goodnight and AJ got ready for bed. While she was on the phone with Khristian, Max had gone back into the kitchen to see if he could hear anything new.

"Well?" AJ said when Max came back into her room.

"Nothing new. Uncle Eric left, and Mema, Papa, and your mom are just talking about what he told them."

AJ's mom came into her room just then. "Who are you talking to?"

"Uh, I was just saying prayers with Max," AJ said.

Her mom said, "Maxie, you're such a good doggie saying your prayers." She reached over and scratched Max's ears, then tucked AJ into bed and left the room.

"Saying prayers with me? That's pretty lame," Max said.

"I couldn't think of anything else real fast. I'm tired, so I guess we'd better really say our prayers. We don't want God mad at us for lying."

The next evening, Uncle Eric got to the house around six o'clock. Charles, Lynn and Buddy showed up at six-thirty. When AJ opened the door to let them in, Buddy immediately ran through the whole house acting crazy while Lynn, AJ, and Max chased after him. When he got to Amy's bedroom and saw the cats, Oreo and Brownie, he decided it was playtime. Oreo hissed at Buddy and hid under the bed. Buddy ran right up to Brownie with his tongue hanging out of his mouth looking like a big doofus.

Brownie, who liked Max OK but didn't really tolerate other dogs, swiped his big red tongue with one of her sharp front claws. Buddy screamed like he'd been shot. He ran back up the hallway yelping and out onto the screened-in porch where he cowered and whimpered. When Lynn caught up to him, she knelt down and tried to comfort the big pup.

"What a dummy," AJ whispered to Max.

"He's not too smart, is he? One look at Brownie should tell any dog that she doesn't suffer fools lightly."

"She does have that mean face. Do you think she hurt him?"

"He outweighs her by forty pounds," Max said. "How could she hurt him?" Brownie was Max's buddy, and he didn't want her to get into trouble because of that dolt, Buddy.

Finally, Buddy stopped whining and started exploring the house again. When he reached the kitchen, he spotted Max's food bowl. He ran right over to it and started chowing down. That was the last straw for Max, and he went snarling after the pup. Each of the girls grabbed her dog's collar and pulled them apart.

"Do you kids think you can keep the dogs and cats under control so the adults can talk?" AJ's mom said. "AJ, take Max to my room and close the door. Lynn, take Buddy to the screened-in porch."

The girls did as they were told. When AJ got to her mom's room, she said, "What's with you—going after poor Buddy just because he ate a few bites of your food? Did you have to act like such a dog?"

"I am a dog!" Max said.

"Oh yeah. Sometimes I forget."

"When you go back in the kitchen, will you please hide my food dish so that pest doesn't eat it all?"

AJ closed Max in her mom's room and went out to the screened-in porch to sit and wait with Lynn.

In the kitchen, Charles, Eric, Amy, Mema and Papa were sitting at the kitchen table.

"Charles, I have some good news and some bad news," Eric said. "The good news is that the local District Attorney is willing to work with you. As long as you cooperate, he'll try to keep you out of jail."

"What's the bad news?" Charles asked.

"Well, my boss has a friend in the Tampa FBI field office. He contacted his friend, off the record, and told him your story. The FBI is very concerned, and they're getting involved. They say that Ali matches the description of a man wanted in connection with a suspected terrorist group. The FBI also wants your full cooperation, but they aren't guaranteeing they won't file charges against you."

Charles rubbed a hand over his face, "Why's that?"

"They said if they find out that you were involved in any terrorist activities, you'll be going to jail."

Charles sat up straight. "I wasn't involved in no terrorist activities—so I don't feel I got nothing to worry about from the FBI."

"I wouldn't say that until you hear what they want from you. First, they want you to give them Ali's cell phone number and the email addresses they're using to send and receive emails."

"Lynn said you'd probably want those, so she copied them down today. She's got 'em."

"That's great! She's a smart girl. I guess that's about all I have for tonight. Can you meet me here again tomorrow night?" Eric asked.

"Long as them guys don't get suspicious."

Eric went to the porch and got the paper from Lynn with the cell phone numbers and email addresses. He and Charles stood and talked for a minute, completing arrangements to meet the next night. Eric and AJ walked Charles, Lynn and Buddy to the front door and saw them out.

Once they'd gone, Eric told Mema, Papa, and Amy he had a few more things to tell them. Max crawled under the kitchen table to listen. AJ had let him out of her mom's room as soon as Charles and Lynn left.

"We're going to be quietly trying to move a few of the neighbors closest to the hellion children's house out of their homes until this is over," he said.

"Won't those men get suspicious if they see people leaving?" Papa asked.

"We're going to have the people spread the news that they're taking long Thanksgiving vacations. Hopefully, if anyone from Charles's house asks about them leaving, they'll hear that."

"What about you guys?" Eric continued. "Do you want to come and stay with Liza and me until all of this is over?"

"Do you think that's necessary?" Mema asked. "Remember how crowded we all were during the hurricane?"

"I certainly would feel better if you weren't here, but to be honest, we kind of need you here for cover, so we can keep meeting with Charles."

"Well, then we'll stay here, at least until you're ready to actually arrest those men," Mema said. Papa and Amy agreed.

"What are we going to do about the Sweeneys?" Amy said. "They're supposed to go away overnight tomorrow, and Khristian is supposed to stay here for the weekend. I know once we tell Amy and Mark what's going on, they won't let Khristian stay here."

"We don't have permission from the FBI to tell anyone else yet. They want everything in this neighborhood looking totally normal. The more people who know what's going on, the bigger the chance of the information leaking and the terrorists hearing about it."

"I don't really feel good about not telling them," Amy said.

"I don't either, but we don't have any other choice."

Eric left and everyone else got ready for bed. Max went into AJ's room and told her about the last conversation.

"Max, I want to stay here and help, I do. But what if those scruffy men find out what's going on and set off some explosions?"

"I guess you have something new to add to your bedtime prayers tonight."

"Very funny. What time is it? Should I call Khristian and let him know what's going on?"

"No, he'll be here tomorrow for the whole weekend. We can tell him everything that's happened then."

Saturday morning, when Amy and AJ got to the bowling alley for YABA Youth League, Khristian ran up and grabbed AJ's wrist. "Come on," he said. "I want to show you something."

He dragged AJ into the arcade under the pretense of showing her a new game. "I'm dying to know what's been happening since Wednesday. Hurry up, tell me."

"I don't know where to start," AJ said. "So much has happened."

At that moment, the two Amys showed up at the arcade door, telling AJ and Khristian that league bowling started in five minutes. It was time to get ready.

"I'll fill you in when we get to my house," AJ whispered.

After bowling, the two moms transferred all of Khristian's stuff for the weekend to Amy's Jeep.

"I sure appreciate this," Khristian's mom said. "It seems like Khristian has been staying at your house every weekend lately. And next weekend, we're all going to the big game. I can't believe you guys got all those tickets."

"We love having Khristian. He keeps AJ busy and then she doesn't bug me so much saying she's bored."

"Hey!" AJ said. "I don't bug you."

AJ and Khristian got into the car and fastened their seat belts. The two Amys were still standing in the parking lot talking.

Khristian said, "I want to hurry up and get to your house so you and Max can tell me what's been going on. Did your uncle get the sheriff involved?"

"Yes, he did. The FBI, too."

"The FBI! Wow!"

When AJ's mom got into the car, she said, "I have a few errands to run."

"Oh, no. Can't you take Khristian and me home first?"

"That would be out of my way. It's only three or four stops. We'll be home soon."

AJ and Khristian looked at each other at the same time and rolled their eyes. That struck them funny, and they both started laughing.

"What's so funny?" Amy said.

"Oh, it's just a kid's joke," AJ said.

When they finally got home, AJ, Khristian, and Max went into AJ's room to talk. AJ turned on her TV to cover the sound of their conversation. After Max and AJ told Khristian everything that had happened for the last two nights, he was excited.

"Let's go for a walk so we can see if any of the neighbors are leaving yet," he said.

"I don't think that's a good idea," AJ said.

"Me either," Max added.

"Why not?" Khristian asked.

"Last night my mom said I can't go over there until this is all over."

"But I don't want to go over there, not to the hellion children's house. Why can't we just take a walk around the neighborhood? Then we could just casually walk past there to see what's happening?"

"I'd really like to, but I don't want to get into trouble."

"Come on, AJ. I can't stand it. I haven't been here to see what's been going on. Just humor me."

"And my mom thinks you're a good influence on me. Little does she know how you egg me on. OK, but we're not stopping at Lynn's house."

"Kids," Max said. "I want to go with you."

"Of course, Max. We wouldn't leave you behind. Are you going so you can keep Khristian and me safe?"

"Partly, even though the adults don't seem to think I'm very good at that," he sniffed. "I really want to see if my special 'doggie' senses can pick up anything."

"I didn't know you had special 'doggie' senses. Is that anything like super powers?" Khristian taunted Max.

"Very funny. Don't make me bite you again."

"OK, OK. I'll be good," Khristian said. "But I'm telling you right now, if you ever bite me again, I'm going to bite you back."

"All you'd get would be a big mouthful of fur," AJ said.

"Yeah, maybe it's time to take you back to Fluffy Cuts," Khristian laughed. That did it, Max jumped up and tried to bite Khristian, who ran into the living room yelling, "Mad dog. Mad dog."

When the kids left the house with Max on his leash, they decided to walk toward the little park instead of toward Lynn's house, just in case one of the adults was watching.

"Do you think the FBI has already contacted any of the neighbors?" Khristian asked.

"I don't know, but it sure seems quiet for a Saturday afternoon, doesn't it?"

"Yeah, I haven't seen anyone outside. Max, are your special 'doggie' senses picking up anything?"

"Khristian, one of these days you're going to push me too far," Max threatened. "But to answer your question, I am not sensing anything. I wonder where all the neighborhood kids are?"

"Maybe they're gone already."

"I doubt that. Uncle Eric just told us last night about the plan to move people. They wouldn't have had time to contact everyone and get them packed up and out of here in less than a day, would they?"

"No, probably not. Hey, there's Lynn at the picnic table. Remember, we can't say anything to her about the FBI's plans to move the neighbors," Max reminded AJ and Khristian. AJ let go of Max's leash, and he ran up to Lynn. She got off the picnic table bench and knelt on the ground to give him a hug.

"What're you doing here?" Khristian asked.

"I was bored. I knew you two were at bowling, and my mom took my brothers to get haircuts. Dad's cleaning the pool, and I just wanted to get away. Something weird has happened."

They're Gone!

"What?" AJ and Khristian asked at once.

"When my dad and I got home last night, those men were gone."

"What do you mean gone?" AJ asked.

"Gone. My mom said they threw some of their things in my dad's old van and left."

"Why didn't you call us and tell us?"

"Because we don't know if they're gone for good or if they're coming back."

"Well, you can't just stay in that house and wait for them. You need to get your family out of there. We need to tell my uncle about this, right away. Come on. Let's go to my house and call him."

"But what if they come back?"

"They might. But what if we could get your family out of there before they do? Then you'd all be safe. Let's run. I have a feeling this is very important."

The three kids ran out of the park and down the street toward AJ's house. Max kept up with them, but he was out of breath by the time they'd gone a block.

"Come on, Max. You're slowing us down." AJ leaned over and unsnapped Max's leash so he could move at his own pace. When they got home, AJ's mom was just coming out of the front door.

"Mom, we have something to tell you," AJ was a little breathless herself. "We need to call Uncle Eric."

"OK. Calm down. What's the matter?" The kids were all leaning over, grasping their knees and trying to catch their breath.

"Try to relax and take a deep breath," AJ's mom said. Of course, AJ, the professional talker, was the first to recover.

"Lynn just told us that when they got home last night, the scruffy men were gone. They took her dad's van and left. They haven't been back since."

"I'll call your uncle. You three go on into the house. I just made some sweet tea. Have a glass and try to calm down. Lynn, is anyone at home at your house?"

"Just my dad. He's cleaning the pool, or he was when I left."

"OK. Go on in with AJ and Khristian."

The rest of the day was a flurry of activity. First, Uncle Eric arrived. He told Lynn that he wanted her to call her house and make sure the men hadn't come back.

Lynn called, and when she hung up the phone, she looked at Uncle Eric. "My dad said the men haven't come back. He also said he tried to use the computer, and they've wiped out the hard drive."

"We've got some squad cars and an FBI forensic van waiting a couple of blocks away. We think the men must have found out somehow that Charles was talking to us and run away. We're going to go into the house and process it for evidence."

He turned to Mema. "Mom, is it OK if Lynn's family comes over here while we process the house?"

Mema said 'Of course," and Eric left.

A few minutes later, everyone in the house heard a dissonant chorus of sirens. They all ran out the front door and walked to the end of the street. There, they watched as the Sheriff's office, FBI, and a couple of unmarked cars and vans converged on Lynn's house.

Within five minutes, Uncle Eric was back. With him were Lynn's mom, Ann, Lynn's three brothers, and of course, Buddy.

"This is going to be a great day with those three delinquents here," Khristian whispered to AJ.

Amy took Lynn's mom inside. Lynn, AJ and Khristian stood facing Lynn's three brothers. The battle lines were drawn.

"What's going on with Dad? Why didn't he come with you?" Lynn asked.

"I heard some Fed say he's being *debriefed*," her oldest brother, Tom said. He pantomimed quote marks with his two index fingers when he said debriefed. "Lynn, what's going on? Dad wouldn't tell us anything. He just said we had to come with AJ's uncle and wait here for him."

Buddy was straining on the leash, trying to get to Lynn, and Lynn's middle brother, Randy was having a hard time controlling him.

Tom reached out to help Randy with Buddy's leash. "Buddy, stop it."

"Whadda you looking at, Pretty Boy?" her youngest brother, John, snarled at Khristian.

"Oh, boy! Here we go," Khristian said under his breath.

"Back off, boys," Lynn warned. "If you do one thing, say one word to start any trouble, I'm going in to tell mom. You know she won't put up with your crap like dad does. The Harveys' are being very nice letting us come over here while all those cops are at our house. If you'll just try to behave for a few minutes, I'll explain what's been going on."

"What *is* going on?" Tom asked. "Does it have anything to do with those weird guys who've been staying at our house?"

AJ said, "I'm going in and get us all something to drink. Why don't we walk down to the park, and we can talk. Khristian, would you put Max back on his leash?"

When AJ came out of the house with six bottles of water, everyone, including the two dogs, was ready to go. There wasn't much conversation on the way to the park. The boys were straining to keep Buddy under control, Lynn was thinking about what to tell her brothers, and Khristian was on guard, waiting for one of the unruly boys to start trouble. AJ was the only one talking, going on about her favorite brand of bottled water. No one was listening to her.

When the group reached the park, Lynn spoke up. "Tom, tie Buddy's leash to the picnic table so we don't have to fight to keep him under control."

While Tom was doing that, AJ unsnapped Max's leash, so he could get away from the unbearable pup.

Lynn patiently explained everything to her brothers. It took a long time, and they had a lot of questions, most of which she couldn't answer.

"I don't know," Lynn answered again. This time, Tom had asked if their dad was going back to jail.

A family of ducks swam by where the kids were sitting near the water, and Buddy jumped up so hard, the whole table bounced.

"We'd probably better get back to the house. When I went in to get the water, Mema said not to stay too long," AJ said.

"Why do you call your grandparents Mema and Papa?" John asked. "That sounds stupid."

"I don't know. It's what I started calling them when I learned to talk, and I've never called them anything else. It is not stupid!" AJ put her hands on her hips and glared at John.

Before more trouble could start, Lynn said, "AJ, you'd better see what that stuff is that Max is rolling in. It can't be good."

AJ ran over to Max. He was lying on his back in a big pile of horse poop, wiggling back and forth. "Max! Gross. How can you do that? You're disgusting."

Max sat up, and Khristian could have sworn he had a big smile on his face. "Whew!" Khristian said. "He stinks."

"Did he get it all over his collar? No? Good. Can you grab his leash and hook him up, Khristian. We're going to have to take him home."

"I'm not touching him. He's your dog."

"Some friend you are." AJ attached Max's leash and jerked it tight. He'd been headed back for the disgusting pile. Lynn's brothers thought this was the funniest thing they'd ever seen.

Randy said, "Our dog might be stupid, but at least he doesn't roll in poop." Randy didn't realize that while they were watching AJ get Max under control, Buddy had slipped his collar.

"*Oh Yeah!* Well think again, mister!" AJ pointed to the pile of poop where Buddy was happily rolling around and acting like he was in doggie heaven.

The kids managed to get the two dogs back to the Harveys, but when they got there, Mema wouldn't let them in the house. She threw the dog shampoo and a brush out the front door and told them to use the garden hose and give both dogs baths.

By the time the two dogs were clean, the six kids needed baths. Lynn's mom took her three sons into the big bathroom, and Lynn went to shower in Amy's bathroom.

Khristian rolled up the garden hose, and AJ gathered up the shampoo and brush. Max shook to rid his fur of the water and soaked both kids again.

"Sorry," he mumbled.

"Max, how could you roll in that stuff? That's the most disgusting thing you've ever done."

"What can I say? The smell was like a magnet right in the middle of my back, drawing me into its powers."

"Not powers—poop. That was just plain ole horse poop. If people have to clean up after their dogs, why don't they have to clean up after their horses?"

"Aren't you going to get a towel and dry me off?" Max asked.

"You don't deserve it."

"Hey! I didn't do anything wrong, I'm a dog."

"You're a talking dog. That makes you almost human. You should be above such disgusting things."

"You're wrong, AJ. I'm not human. I'm a dog. You're right, I'm a dog that talks, but I'm still a dog. Just because I chose to talk to you because you're in danger, that doesn't change what I am. I'm a dog." Max tossed his head and walked to the porch and sat in front of the door.

"I think you hurt his feelings," Khristian said.

"I think you're right. It was just so disgusting."

"You already said that. You need to go talk to him. He's risked everything to help us. You shouldn't have talked to him like that."

AJ hung her head. Khristian was right. She walked over to Max and gave him a hug, not caring that she was getting soaked again. "I'm sorry, Max. I love you."

Max gave her a big kiss on the cheek. "I love you too, AJ." He stood up, wagging his tail and waiting to be let in.

About the time all the kids finished showering, Charles arrived from his debriefing, and Mema said dinner was ready. Everyone was eating dessert when Uncle Eric came back to the house.

"Charles, when your family is through eating, we're going to take you back to your house to pack some things. We don't feel it's safe for your family to stay there right now. There are two federal officers waiting outside. Once you're packed, they'll take your family somewhere they feel is safe."

"How long are we gonna hafta stay there?"

"No one is sure right now. They're going to take your computer back to the lab and have one of their experts try to retrieve what was erased from the hard drive. Hopefully, we'll have a better idea after that."

While Charles and Ann were thanking all the Harveys for their help, Khristian and AJ were talking to Lynn.

"You know we have plans for the game next Saturday. We still want you to go with us," AJ told Lynn.

"I want to go. It sounds like fun. If they'll let us use a phone, I'll call you to see what the arrangements are. AJ, thank you, and you too, Khristian. You're probably the best friends I've ever had." She gave both of them hugs. Khristian's face turned cherry red.

Boys! AJ thought.

The Big Game or the Big Boom

It was another busy week, with school, youth group, lessons, and plans for the big game. Mema and Papa had borrowed a friend's motor home, and Mema's cousin Jon and Cathy had borrowed his mom's motor home. All their friends and family who were going to the game were leaving on Friday afternoon. They would camp overnight in the RVs, and take them to the stadium for tailgate parties the next day before the game.

Uncle Eric made arrangements to pick up Lynn from the safe house so that she could attend the game. Even the dogs were going, because no one would be left at home to care for them.

Thursday night, about seven o'clock, the doorbell rang. When AJ answered the door, it was Tia Dora and JJ.

"Hi, Tia Dora. Hi, JJ." Alyssa gave the German Shepherd's ears a scratch.

"AJ, I have a family emergency. We have to go to Georgia tonight. My mother-in-law is very ill. I need a favor?"

"Sure. What can I do for you?"

"Can you keep JJ for us? We can't take him with us. Our car is too small."

"Come on in. I need to ask my mom and Mema and Papa.

"We're all leaving tomorrow in two RVs to go to the Gator-Seminole game. We're already taking four dogs," AJ said. "We're taking Max. Uncle Eric and Aunt Liza are bringing Misha and Mick, and Jon and Cathy are bringing their little yorkie. Her name is Gator because John and Cathy are Gator fans, too. But Mema calls her Yapper because she never shuts up."

"Oh, that's too much. I can't ask you to take JJ, too," Tia Dora said. But Mema had come into the room while Tia Dora and AJ were talking, and she said for Dora not to worry about it, they would take JJ. When Tia Dora protested, Mema said, "We're so used to chaos and confusion in this family. What's one more dog?"

So that's how JJ came to be in Gainesville with everyone.

The day of the big game, the weather was perfect. The temperature was sixty-eight degrees with low humidity and a slight breeze. The family needed every inch of space in the two borrowed motor homes. The total number attending the game was eight adults, four kids, and five dogs, including JJ, and one pest, Jamie.

"Max," Misha said. "Who's your handsome friend?"

"Mick, Misha, this is JJ. He's a retired ATF police dog and a neighbor of ours. His people had to go out of town, so he's staying with us."

"Cool," Mick said. "Did you ever get to chase bad guys? Did you get to attack them? Did you ever sniff out any dope? How about bombs? Have you ever ridden in a helicopter . . . ?"

"Mick, Mick. Settle down, boy. I'm sure JJ has done all those things. And we'd love to hear all about it, wouldn't we, boys?" Misha was practically purring.

Max had never heard her sound so nice when talking to another dog. Was she batting her eyes at JJ?

JJ didn't seem to notice. "Well, my buddy Max was with me on my most recent adventure. I smelled plastic explosives in a house right in our neighborhood."

"Was that where the scruffy men were, Max? The reason you had to break the Animal Code of Silence and tell the kids they were in danger?" Mick asked. His head whipped around, "Misha, what's wrong with your eyes?" he went on.

"Nothing. Please go on, JJ. Tell us *all* about it."

I've never seen her act so silly, Max thought.

JJ told Mick and Misha how Max and the kids had taken him to the hellion children's house to check for explosives. They were both quite impressed. Misha thought she might even have to reevaluate how she'd been treating Max.

The door was thrown open, and AJ, Khristian, Lynn, and AJ's friend Allie came into the RV.

"Come on puppies," AJ called. "It's time for a last walk before the game starts." AJ's friend Allie, actually another Alyssa, took Max, Lynn took JJ, AJ led Mick, and Khristian, because he was the strongest, took Misha, who generally never behaved on a leash. No one volunteered to take Gator, because the little dog was a pain in the neck, even if she was cute.

The kids headed toward the far end of the parking lot. Khristian said, "I can't believe how well Misha is behaving. She usually barks at other dogs, whines, and growls and pulls on the leash so hard I feel like she's trying to pull my arms out of the sockets."

"I think she's in love," AJ said. "She hasn't left JJ's side since we started off."

"I'm glad you didn't put that awful muzzle on JJ," Lynn said. "He's really a very well-behaved dog. I can't believe Royanne convinced everyone he's dangerous."

"He'd have to be well-behaved to be a police dog," Khristian added. "They don't allow disobedient dogs. If you ask me, Royanne is the one who needs a muzzle." Everyone laughed.

"How long until the game starts? I don't want to miss kick-off," AJ said.

"We have plenty of time. It's only one-fifteen. The game doesn't start for another forty-five minutes."

AJ decided to tease Allie. "Misha's not the only one who's in love. What about Allie and Zack?"

"You said you wouldn't say anything about that," Allie said.

The kids continued walking the dogs, not paying any attention to the time. They were too busy talking and teasing each other about school, boyfriends and girlfriends and such. But that ended when AJ noticed that the parking lot was almost empty of people.

"Khristian, we should probably turn back now. It looks like most of the people are heading into the stadium," AJ said.

"OK," Khristian said and looked at his watch. "Hey! We'd better hurry. The game starts in twenty minutes." The kids stopped and got the dogs turned around to start back.

"Maybe I spoke too soon about JJ being so well-behaved," Lynn said. Instead of turning back with everyone else, JJ was straining on his leash, dragging Lynn through a row of parked cars. When he reached an old van, he jumped up and started scratching at the rear door and growling. The van looked like it had been painted by hand. It was Gator blue and orange with big cartoon Gator emblems on its side panels.

AJ handed Mick's leash to Khristian and went to help Lynn. She thought that since JJ was more familiar with her, she would have an easier time getting him under control.

"JJ, come on, boy. It's OK." But JJ continued whining and scratching at the van door. In a firmer voice, AJ commanded, "JJ, down!" The retired police dog sat, but he wouldn't budge, and he wouldn't stop whining. AJ tried pulling on his collar, but suddenly, Lynn grabbed her arm and told her to stop.

"What? If the people who own this van come back, they'll be mad at us," AJ complained.

"I own this van," Lynn said.

"What do you mean?" Khristian asked.

"Well, it's been painted, but I'd know this van anywhere. This is my dad's old van. See that dent in the back fender? My brother Tom did that. He was trying to hit John with a baseball bat."

"Why doesn't that surprise me?" Khristian mumbled under his breath.

"Lynn, are you sure?" Ali asked. She was now having a hard time with Max, who uncharacteristically was straining on his leash, trying to get to JJ.

"I'm sure. AJ, even you should remember this cracked window . . . Oh no! Remember those cops said they thought the scruffy men might have put explosives in the van?"

"How could I forget? Lynn, are you really sure this is the same van?" AJ said.

"I can prove it. If this is my dad's van, there'll be one of those magnetic key boxes under the back left fender. My mom was always losing her keys." Lynn knelt down and reached into the tire-well. She felt around for a minute, then pulled her dirt-covered fist out. She turned her hand over and opened it. There on her palm was a magnetic key box.

"Oh, my gosh! Now what do we do?" AJ said. "I wish one of us had a cell phone so we could call my uncle."

"Your grandfather said if you get straight As, he'd get you one."

"I know, but I got that B in math."

Meanwhile, Lynn opened the tin box and took out the key. She fit it into the lock in one of the back door handles."

"Lynn, I wouldn't open that door. What if there are explosives in there? They could be rigged to blow up if the door is opened. Look how JJ's acting."

Before Khristian could finish what he was saying, Lynn turned the key and opened the back door. JJ yelped and jumped up into the back of the old van. He ran over to a large cardboard box, growling and sniffing.

"Guys," Allie said, "I don't think this is such a good idea." She was pulling on Max's leash and backing away from the van.

Khristian was still holding onto the leashes for both Misha and Mick, and he couldn't get close enough to see into the van. "What do you see?" he asked.

"Well, it looks empty except for an old cardboard box," Lynn said. She climbed into the van and walked over to the box, which was upside down. She lifted it up. "Uh oh! What's this?"

AJ finally noticed Max straining to get to the van. "Allie, let go of Max," she commanded. Allie dropped Max's leash, and he ran to the back of the van and jumped in.

"I wish I had a cell phone," AJ said again.

"Well, you don't. So stop whining. What are we going to do?" Allie sounded very frightened.

"Allie, would you mind going back to the RVs? Tell the adults what we've found, and bring them back here as soon as possible. If you wouldn't mind, could you take Mick and Misha with you?" Allie grabbed the leashes for Mick and Misha from Khristian, turned around and started running back in the direction of the RVs.

"Man, do you think she was in a hurry to get out of here, or what?" Khristian said.

"Lynn, maybe you should come down out of there. It could be dangerous." Lynn seemed to consider this for a minute. Then she made a decision and climbed down from the back of the van.

"Allie isn't going to be able to go very fast with those dogs. I ran track last year. I'm going to run and get some help."

"That's a great idea," AJ said. "I'll stay here and keep JJ and Max under control."

When Lynn left, AJ said to Max, "Max, find out why JJ is so upset. Are there explosives in this van?"

Khristian climbed up into the van with Max and JJ while AJ stood at the open back door.

"Max," Khristian said, "what is it?"

Max said, "JJ says he definitely smells explosives. You know, it smells the same as the garage at the hellion children's house—even to my untrained nose."

Khristian passed the news on to AJ.

"Oh, my gosh! What do we do now? Should we run, or what?" AJ was wringing her hands.

Khristian knelt over what looked like a metal box of some kind. "What are you looking at?" AJ asked him.

"I'm not sure. There are some switches, and some big red numbers—like a digital readout on this top panel."

"Let JJ get a good look at it and see if he's ever seen anything like it before," AJ said.

Khristian called the German shepherd over. JJ was very skittish. "Geez, JJ," Khristian said. "Be careful. We don't want to set anything off."

JJ inched across the floor on his stomach, like a movie dog who'd been wounded. When he was next to Khristian, he communicated to Max. *Danger! Danger! Must get away!*

"JJ, have you ever seen anything like this before?" Max asked.

"Danger, Max. Take human children away. We need to run. I don't like this."

"I know. It's dangerous. You said that. But we need to know if this thing is getting ready to go off," Max said.

Just then, some Florida State fans were walking by. They banged on the Gator emblem on the side of the van with their fists. "*Boo, Gators. Go, Seminoles.*" They hooted.

Max jumped two feet off the floor of the van. "Was that thunder?"

JJ yelped and jumped out the back door of the van.

"Geez, they scared me to death," AJ said. "When they pounded on the side of the van, I thought that thing went off. Don't you think the adults must be wondering where we are by now? The parking lot's almost empty."

Max walked to the back of the van and said to JJ, "Please try to think back. Surely in all your years as an ATF dog, you must have seen something like this."

AJ didn't realize she was holding her breath until Max said, "JJ says he thinks it's a time bomb."

"A time bomb! Khristian, come down out of there," AJ yelled.

"AJ, if it's a time bomb, we need to find out when it's set to go off," Khristian said. "Let me watch these red numbers for a minute and see if I can tell anything."

Against her better judgment, AJ climbed into the back of the van with Khristian and Max. She crawled over and knelt next to Khristian, who pointed to an LED readout.

"See these numbers? I wonder if they have something to do with when this thing is supposed to go off.

Max walked to the back of the van and said to JJ, "Are you afraid?"

Of course, I'm afraid. There's a bomb in there. JJ was cowering on the ground, shaking.

"But you worked for ATF for years. You helped find lots of bombs. I can't believe you're so scared.

I found them and then I left. The men disarmed them. I didn't have to stay in the danger.

The dogs were interrupted when AJ gasped. As she and Khristian were peering at the numbers on the metal box—a big red one and zero—the one disappeared, and the zero changed to a nine." "I sure hope that means nine hours," AJ said.

"We were only watching for about a minute when it changed. I hate to tell you—it must mean nine minutes."

"Nine minutes? We're gonna die," JJ said to Max.

"Nine minutes? There are supposed to be over 80,000 people here today. We can't get help and get out of here in nine minutes," AJ said.

"Probably only eight and a half by now," Khristian answered.

"JJ," Max said. Do you know how to disarm this thing?"

"I'm only trained to sniff them out, not disarm them. I keep telling you, once I find them, my job's over. I should probably be getting back now."

"Very funny," Max said sarcastically. "Please try to think back, JJ. Surely in all your years as an ATF dog, you must have seen something like this. Maybe as part of a training exercise?"

"What'd he say, Max?" Khristian asked.

"He said we're on our own. Are there any tools in here?"

Both kids felt around the floor of the van. Under a piece of carpet, AJ found a screwdriver. In another corner, Khristian found some pliers.

"We could at least get the cover off of this thingie. Then when help comes, it won't take them so long," AJ said.

"Thingie?"

"Well, I'm not comfortable calling it a bomb. I feel like if I say it's a bomb, it will really be a bomb."

"I guess getting the cover off makes sense. Give me that screwdriver. I only see four screws," Khristian said.

"Khristian, we can't do this," AJ wailed. "Our moms won't even let us cross Keene Road by ourselves."

"AJ, there isn't anyone else," Max said. "Paws don't work well with tools. Khristian, do you think you can loosen the screws?"

"Probably, but do you really think that's a good idea?"

"It could save time." Max looked around when JJ jumped back into the van.

"And JJ said you need to be very careful—do not bump anything."

"Great! Don't bump anything. Max, if you think thunder is loud, it's nothing compared to what this bomb would sound like if it went off."

"No jokes. Just concentrate," Max warned.

Khristian *was* concentrating—very hard. He placed the head of the screwdriver into the slot on the first screw and tried to turn it, but it wouldn't budge. He sat back on his heels.

"I'm scared," he said.

"Me, too," AJ answered.

"AJ, this might be a good time for a prayer. We need all the help we can get. Khristin, try again, a little bit more pressure this time, but remember, no jerky motions." Max spoke to the two children in a very low, calming voice.

AJ tried to pray, "Father God, in the name of your son, Jesus . . ." she stopped and took a deep breath. "God, I don't know what to say. We're scared, and we need your help. We don't want anyone to get hurt, but we don't know what do to. Could you please send us some help? We really love you and everything, but I don't think our moms would be too happy if we came to live with you today. Amen."

"Funny!" Khristian said. He slowly lifted out the first screw and moved to the second.

Earlier, at the computer lab in the sheriff's office, FBI agent Dan Iverson was working on the computer hard drive taken from the hellion children's house the week before. He and Uncle Eric's computer nerd friend, Mike, had pulled quite a lot of information from the damaged hard drive.

Special agent Iverson called over to Mike, "I just recovered some information that could really be significant."

"What do you have?"

"You know that so far, most of the stuff we've pulled has to do with a series of coordinated events planned for New Years Day?"

"Right," Mike answered.

"Well, this is different. I found some research regarding the annual football game between Florida and Florida State. I also found an email that indicates the terrorists at the house in Largo needed to make a run for it. It sounds like they were thinking about using the Florida—Florida State game as a test. They've got information in here about how many people will be attending the game, how the new addition to the stadium is constructed, all kinds of stuff like that. When is that game?"

"Today," Mike said. "And Deputy Harvey and his whole family are there, including the young girl from the house where we recovered the computer. Harvey picked her up at the safe house this morning."

"Where are you going?" Iverson yelled as Mike ran across the lab.

"I've got Harvey's cell phone number on my desk. I have to call and warn him. You call the Gainesville FBI field office and let them know what you've found. Have them get a bomb squad out to that stadium, and fire trucks—and ambulances. If that thing goes off, a lot of people are going to get hurt." Both men picked up telephones and urgently began making calls.

"Khristian, these pliers have wire cutters," AJ said.

Khristian removed the second screw from the metal frame, but didn't look up at AJ. "How would you know that?" he asked. He gingerly placed the screwdriver in the slot of the third screw head.

"I know because Mema has some pliers just like this. She uses the wire cutters when she's making silk flower arrangements, you know, to cut the stems of the flowers that are too long."

Khristian removed the third screw, and began on the fourth.

"When you get that cover off, if we see a wire in there, maybe we can use the wire cutters to cut it and stop the bomb from going off," AJ said.

"I sure hope we don't have to do that," Khristian replied. "Would you look out the back of the van and see if the adults are coming yet. This thing says four minutes."

AJ stood up and walked to the back of the van. She searched in the direction where the RVs were parked, but she couldn't see the RVs from here. She didn't see anyone she knew, just some more rowdy Florida State fans about five rows over, coming toward the van. They were heading for the stadium entrance.

Khristian removed the last screw. He set the screwdriver down and sat back.

Max said, "Now see if you can lift that metal cover straight up. If you feel anything holding it, don't pull," Max said. "Just set it back in place."

"AJ, would you help me? If we each take hold of two corners, we can keep it level."

AJ knelt across from Khristian. Each child placed a hand under each of two corners of the metal cover. "On the count of three."

They slowly, carefully lifted the metal cover straight up.

"Do you feel anything holding it?" Khristian asked.

Without looking up, AJ answered, "No. How about you?"

"Me neither. Let's lift it off."

They completely removed the boxy cover and laid it next to the bomb.

"It's definitely a bomb, Max," JJ communicated.

There were several bricks of stuff that looked like Play Doh, and wires—way too many wires. How would they know which one to cut?

JJ said to Max, "I do remember something. "

"What? Max said. "Anything that might be helpful."

"I used to work with this guy, they called him Lucky. He said, 'If you're ever in doubt, cut the yellow wire'."

"Are you sure? I was watching Extreme Makeover last week, and they were rewiring an old house. They said the power is always in the red wire," Max questioned.

This isn't a house, it's a bomb.

Eric hung up the phone. All the adults were waiting together outside the RVs. As soon as the kids got back with the dogs, they could go into the game.

He was just starting to tell everyone why Mike had called, when Lynn came running up, with Allie, Mick, and Misha about a hundred yards behind her.

Panting, Lynn tried to tell Eric what they'd found. "Van . . . my dad's van," was all she could get out. She leaned over and grabbed her knees, gasping for breath.

Allie ran up to the group with Mick and Misha who were excited to see everyone. They were barking and whining, adding to the confusion.

Eric leaned over to Lynn, "Are you saying you found your dad's van?" She shook her head and pointed back toward the direction she and Allie had come from. "Painted," she wheezed, "like Gator colors."

"Where are AJ and Khristian?" Amy asked.

"Van," she huffed. "Something in it . . . bomb."

Since Eric hadn't had a chance to explain to everyone about Mike's phone call, this news brought pandemonium to the group. Everyone started talking at once, demanding to know what was going on.

Mema gave Lynn a bottle of water. "Let her get her breath," she said. "Here, drink this, maybe then you can talk."

Overhead, an FBI helicoptor flew by, and the group could hear sirens—lots of sirens. The emergency teams poured into the parking lot. Eric's cell phone rang again.

"This is Harvey."

"Harv, it's Mike. Is help there yet?"

"Looks like they're just arriving. Mike, the kids found the van. It sounds like there might be a bomb in it."

"Talk to Special Agent Brown. He's with the bomb squad. They should be there in a minute. Until he arrives and we can use his radio, stay on your cell phone. You need to direct the bomb squad to that van."

"Is one of you people, Harvey?" a tall good-looking man in an FBI windbreaker asked.

"I'm Harvey, are you Special Agent Brown?" Eric asked.

Eric explained to the FBI agent what Lynn had told him. Then he turned back to Lynn, who was sitting on the step of the RV drinking the water.

"Do you think you can take us to where the van is?" She nodded and got up. She turned and started running back toward the van. Special Agent Brown started after her, and Eric ran behind him. Soon, the whole group of adults was running after Lynn, and the bomb squad was behind them. It was like a big untidy parade.

"Maybe we should run," AJ said.

"I think it's way too late for that," Khristian said. "The timer says one minute."

"Kids, I know this is hard, but we have to do something." Max pushed his nose into AJ's hand. She put her arm around his neck.

"What, Max? What can we do? We're just kids."

"You have to cut one of those wires and see if that timer stops."

"Which one?" Khristian said. "You and JJ can't even agree. You say red, he says yellow."

"Red and yellow make orange. Cut the orange one," AJ said.

I don't have a good feeling about this, Max.

"I don't either, JJ. But we can't just sit here and let this thing go off."

"I'll do it, Max." Khristian said. AJ handed him the wire cutters. The wires were all mingled close together, and there wasn't much slack in them. Khristian carefully worked the wire cutters around the orange wire.

"Let me check one more time to see if anyone is coming," AJ said. She walked to the back and looked out. "Sorry," she said. "I don't see anyone."

"Thirty seconds."

"Father, God, we could sure use that help—now!"

"On the count of three," Max said. "One, Two . . .

Time seemed to stop, and then—everything happened at once.

"No! Don't!" AJ screamed. The rowdy group of Florida State fans was standing at the side of the van, getting ready to rock it. They screamed, "Go, Noles!"

" . . . Three"

The van jolted.

The wire cutters slipped.

Khristian cut the red wire.

Nothing happened.

They waited.

And nothing happened.

Khristian stood, the wire cutters still in his hand. AJ walked over and hugged him. He even hugged her back. Both children had tears in their eyes.

"I'm so proud of you two," Max said. "You did it." They both knelt down and included Max in the hug. Then JJ walked over as if to say, "Don't forget me."

Khristian jumped up and screamed "Boom!" and hit the side of the van with his fist. JJ wet on the floor. Max jumped like he'd been shot. Khristian laughed. "Don't worry, Max. It's not thunder." AJ punched Khristian.

"Khristian," Max said, "One of these days . . ."

AJ started laughing too. Then, time started again, and Uncle Eric and everyone else arrived. It was pandemonium.

Men in windbreakers grabbed the two children and whisked them away from the van.

"It's OK," AJ said. "Khristian cut the wire."

"He what?"

"He cut the wire. We had to. The timer said one minute. We had to do something."

Amy pulled AJ and Khristian away from the special agents. She hugged them like she would never let them go.

Max joined them, giving everyone he could reach big, wet, sloppy kisses.

One of the bomb squad members climbed down from the van. "They did it," he said. "They stopped it. I can't believe it. A couple of kids!"

"How did you know which wire to cut?" another guy said. "There are a bunch of bogus wires here. They were probably trying to cause confusion in case anyone found the bomb before it went off."

"I think we had help from upstairs," AJ pointed heavenward.

Much later, in fact the first half was already over, the happy group of family and friends entered the stadium. Some cheered the Gators. Some cheered the Seminoles. None could stop smiling.

What Now?

Later that week, Uncle Eric came to AJ's house to talk to everyone. He'd told Amy to have Khristian and Allie, Tia Dora and Frank and JJ there. They made it a party to celebrate being alive.

"Didn't you bring Lynn?" AJ asked Uncle Eric when he came into the house.

"I'm sorry, honey. I'll explain about that in a minute. Can you get everyone to gather in the living room so I can talk to them?"

AJ and Khristian looked at each other, rolled their eyes and started laughing.

"What?" Uncle Eric said.

"Well, it's not easy to get everyone together in this house. But we'll try."

About fifteen minutes later, everyone gathered in the living room. No play this time.

Uncle Eric got everyone's attention and started talking.

"First, I'm sorry Lynn couldn't be here. But since the terrorists that were at her house haven't been caught, she and her family are now in the witness protection program. You won't be seeing them because they've been moved to another state."

There were a few groans. AJ said, "I'll miss Lynn."

Khristian said, "Yippie! The hellion children are gone." His mom gave him a dirty look. "Well, that's what Mema calls them," he explained.

"I have some good news, though," Uncle Eric said.

"The FBI bureau was very impressed with our children." Max bumped Bubbie's leg with his head. "Sorry, Max. And our dogs." JJ came to sit next to Max. Everyone laughed.

"They would like to give the kids medals." Max bumped his leg again. "And the dogs. Max, sometimes I think you're human."

AJ and Khristian grabbed hands and started dancing around the living room. "Medals!" AJ said.

"We'll be famous," Khristian added.

"Well, not really," Uncle Eric said.

"What, no medals?"

"Yes, medals. No, famous. You see, kids, it's too dangerous. Those guys are still out there. The bureau is afraid that if they publicize what happened, they might come after you. So, you will receive medals. I even heard the Governor might give them to you. And both universities were so grateful, they've both offered scholarships to whichever of the two you choose. But it will have to be in a private ceremony."

"That's OK," AJ said. "We're just happy this is over. No more mysteries for us, right Khristian?"

Coming Soon—AJ and Friends: The Secret Tunnel

AJ and Max are spending the summer with AJ's cousins in Illinois. The children are given a summer project to research the history of the small Illinois town at the local library. There, they happen upon the story of an old coal tunnel that begins in the sandstone bluffs north of town, traverses beneath the Illinois River, and exits in the hills south of town.

Curiosity causes the children to search for the old tunnel entrance which is close to where AJ's cousins live. They discover someone has been in the tunnel recently. The walls are shorn up, there are battery-operated lights installed, and the under-river passage has been reopened. Max's spidey senses are on high alert; he senses danger.

Join Max, AJ, Paige and Joe as they explore the reason for the danger.